Survivor

SEARCH FOR MEANING

A Novel By

Steve Badger

ISBN-13: 978-1505753998

ISBN-10: 1505753996

Dedication
This novel is dedicated to every person
who is still searching for reality with God.

Trust God to make your search successful;
He wants you to succeed.

Acknowledgments

Special thanks to these friends for helping me by reading and commenting on the story and finding typos: Jack Bedenbaugh, Timothy Badger, and Hope Gonzalez.

Table of Contents

Preface

By definition, a novel is fiction, and this novel is no different. Almost all of the characters and the churches are products of my imagination. However, I hope that this fictional story is true in the sense that it reflects reality.

A few of the books, authors, and artists mentioned are real, and readers may want to consult some of them. A list of the authors and titles of their books and articles, and entertainers are at the end of the book. *Survivor: Search for Meaning* attempts to chronicle the reality that so many people around the world have found in the Gospel of Christ Jesus for centuries.

The characters in the novel are not portrayed as perfect people who always use holy language or make godly choices. But Adam's experiences—with the exception of his amnesia—are similar to those of millions of people around the world.

As you read, I hope you will reflect on how God has revealed himself to you in your life and how you have responded to that divine revelation.

January 2015
Steve Badger
Seminary, MS
docbadger@gmail.com

Chapter 1: Saved

The jet plane crashed in a sparsely wooded pasture about halfway between Dallas and Waco, spreading forty-one bodies, luggage, and aircraft debris over half a mile of Texas farmland. Daylight was fading as the first responders arrived at the crash scene—not that daylight or time would have made any difference in the number of fatalities. As soon as they surveyed the wreckage, half a dozen experienced EMTs were certain they would find no survivors.

Fully loaded, the plane could hold forty-five passengers and a crew of four. The flight from Love Field to Houston would take about an hour. Suitcase debris and small parts of the airplane fuselage were strewn all over the cow pasture.

About thirty minutes after they arrived at the crash site, the investigators expanded their search a little further away from the debris field. One of them whistled and shouted, "Over here, Captain, quick!" While he did not have an official title or rank of captain, all of his crew called him Captain as an affectionate nickname based on his rank in the US Army—and the admiration and respect his crew had for him. Several men immediately started running toward the alarm. The beams from their flashlights produced a bizarre spine-chilling dance in the darkness.

When he was just two or three yards away, Captain shouted, "What is it, Tom? What do you have?" Tom answered by pointing his flashlight beam behind him, revealing the reason for his excitement. In just a moment the other investigators arrived and stared silently when they saw a man lying there apparently in shock.

The victim was well over six feet tall, six-five or six-six. People often used the phrase 'rugged good looks' to describe him or they compared him to Tom Selleck. His facial hair was so heavy, dark, and fast growing that he often shaved twice a day.

Since the man appeared conscious, Captain began questioning him. "What's your name, sir? Tell me your name, please." But the man had a blank face and did not respond. Captain thought, *this person could not have been on that airplane. Maybe he's a terrorist and shot the plane down.* "You men spread out and comb this area," Captain ordered his team.

"What are we looking for, Captain?"

He said, "No idea." But then he offered an idea: "Maybe a rocket launcher. Flag anything bigger than a cigarette butt. If you see anything out of place, don't touch it. This could be part of a crime scene. Tom, stay here with us."

"Yes, sir."

Captain repeated his request to the survivor, "Sir, what's your name?"

The confused man's voice was weak, "I'm sorry. I can't remember. Maybe Caroline—I'm not sure." His eyes remained closed as he spoke.

"No, it's not Caroline—trust me. But it could be Carroll. Is your name Carroll?"

"Maybe. That sounds right."

The captain pointed to the flames and debris field behind him as he asked, "Were you on the plane that crashed?"

The man tried to stand as he said, "No," then "maybe," and then "I don't know."

"Are you injured?"

He tried to reply, "I think so. I feel like I'm..." and then he fell unconscious to the ground. Neither Tom nor Captain tried to catch him until he was on the ground.

Looking down at him, Captain said, "Examine him for injuries, Tom—especially check his head for bleeding." While Tom examined the unconscious stranger, Captain searched the stranger's pockets for a billfold. He found a driver's license with a mug shot and confirmed it matched the stranger.

"Adam Bowers, Plano. He has nine C-notes in his wallet—and some smaller bills too. You find any injuries, Tom?"

"No, sir. Nothing so far. He could not have been on that plane and survive the crash. How did he get here?"

"I agree. Until we know more about him, we better treat him as a criminal suspect." Captain then called to his crew, "Somebody bring a stretcher. Carry this man to an ambulance—Pronto!"

Captain walked with the stretcher to the ambulance. While EMTs were working with Adam, Captain's smart phone beeped, indicating the arrival of an email. He opened it and saw that it had an attachment. "Finally. What took them so long?" The attachment was a passenger manifest, which he opened immediately. The names were in alphabetical order, so he did not have to search far. "Well Tom, the manifest says he was a passenger on that plane, Tom. He's Adam Bowers, and he was seated in 3A—first class." His eyebrows went up as he said the last two words.

Tom said, "That has to be wrong, Captain."

"Yeah. No way he was on that plane. Impossible."

The EMTs who examined him decided that Adam was in shock, moved him to a gurney, and gave him an IV. Adam kept his eyes closed as if he were asleep. Even though the EMTs could not find an injury, they transported him to a nearby hospital in Waco for evaluation. Doctors at the hospital were unable to decide what to do with Adam. They were skeptical that he was on the airplane that crashed, and they transferred him to the hospital's psychiatric wing for observation and evaluation—security provided by a US marshal.

Diana Norris had just finished eating dinner while watching her recording of yesterday's "Jeopardy" and "Wheel of Fortune." As she shut off the DVR and was about to shut off the TV, she noticed the local newscast was reporting a plane crash just southeast of Waco. Her sister and her sister's fiancé had boarded a plane about four hours earlier, so she listened very intently to the news.

She was alone in her apartment north of Dallas and decided to postpone sleep. Instead, she called the airline and quickly established that Adam and Caroline's flight had crashed—and all passengers were believed dead. She was so numb with disbelief and anxiety over this tragedy that she was not watching the TV when a picture of Adam came on the screen. The announcer said that this person, identified as Adam Bowers, was found near the wreckage, alive and unscathed. When she heard "Adam Bowers," she opened her eyes, spun around, and saw his picture. She booted her tablet, searched the Internet for the Waco hospital phone number, and called, but it took several minutes to get connected to someone who would talk to her.

After what seemed like an eternity, a voice said, "This is Dr. Bailey, how may I help you?"

"Dr. Bailey, I'm Diana Norris. Adam Bowers is engaged to my sister, Caroline Norris. They were both on the plane that crashed. I saw on the TV news that Adam Bowers is in the hospital in Waco. I'm trying to find out if he is okay. Is he with you? Have you examined him?"

"Ms Norris, are you his parent, guardian, or spouse?"

"No, sir. I am his fiancée's sister.

"Ma'am, I'm sorry. Federal privacy laws prevent me from divulging any information without a patient's consent."

"I understand. May I speak to Adam on the phone?"

"I cannot confirm that he's here—even to blood relatives. I'm sorry, ma'am. I would have to violate Federal law to help you."

"What do you suggest I do, sir?"

"Are you able to come down to Waco?"

"Yes, I can come right now. I live in Plano, on the north side of Dallas. I can leave in five or ten minutes."

"I think it's too late—I'm about to leave the hospital. If you'll get here tomorrow morning with some photo ID and proof of your relationship to Mr. Bowers and Caroline Norris, we'll try to go from there. Okay? I'm not sure what privacy laws will allow me to do, but we'll try to help."

"Can you at least confirm that he has no life threatening injuries?"

"Ma'am, what did the TV news report?"

"They said he was unscathed."

"Other than shock and some confusion, I'd say that's pretty accurate. Let me give you my cell number." When that task was finished, he said, "Good night, ma'am."

"Thank you. Goodbye." She hung up her phone and started planning for the trip south.

The next day, Diana was headed south on Interstate 35E at five A.M. She passed the geodesic dome church in Waxahachie about six o'clock and was parking the car in front of the hospital at Waco about seven.

She found the hospital cafeteria and bought some breakfast. When she sat down, she used her phone to take a selfie and send it to the cell phone number Dr. Bailey gave her last night—along with two words: 'Diana cafeteria.'

In about 15 minutes—after she'd eaten three over easy eggs, grits, a sausage patty, and a biscuit—a tall middle-aged man walked up to her. He noticed that her eyes looked like she'd been crying. "Ms. Norris?"

She turned her head toward him and replied, "Dr. Bailey?"

"Yes, may I sit down?"

"Please do."

Diana continued drinking her coffee while Dr. Bailey examined the documents she'd brought.

"Have you heard any word about your sister, ma'am?"

"Only indirectly. Official word is all persons on board are presumed dead. I'm waiting for a call from the airline confirming that and helping me to make arrangements for her remains."

"In a moment I'll ask you to follow me to a hospital's psychiatric ward. I'll ask you to confirm or deny that this person is Adam Bowers. Would you do that for us?"

"Yes. But do you have his wallet? It has a Texas driver's license in it, with a photo."

"Yes. We've seen it. We just need to confirm that it's not counterfeit. We think it's genuine. But we have some questions we cannot answer."

"Sure."

"Are you certain that he was on that flight?"

"I watched both of them board that airplane. I saw the plane take-off. Why?"

"We find it absurd that he was on the plane that crashed and escaped without a mark on him. So we're continuing our investigation."

She finished her coffee, and Dr. Bailey took her tray to the conveyor belt. She followed him to an elevator and down a long hall to a secure door into a smaller examination room. As soon as she saw him she said, "Adam Bowers." The man turned his head to see her, but there was no look of recognition on his face.

"Do I know you? Are you Caroline?"

"No, I'm Diana. Caroline is my sister." She wanted to ask him if Caroline had died, but she guessed he would not know.

Diana did not notice the plainclothes sheriff's deputy in the room until she asked, "Ma'am, I'm Deputy Miller. Can you positively identify that he is Adam Bowers?"

"I've known this man for about two years, and the only name I've ever heard him use was Adam Bowers. He works at Terry Realty in Plano. I went by his home and picked up some mail for you." She handed him some mail addressed to Adam Bowers. "If this is an alias, I have no knowledge of it."

Then the deputy asked Diana for her driver's license, and she copied information into her tiny notebook, including Diana's cell phone number. A few moments later, Diana's cell phone rang. The screen showed the number of the incoming call, but no name. Mystified, she answered, "This is Diana."

A voice said, "This is Deputy Miller in Waco." Diana looked across the room and saw the deputy smiling and waving to her, "I just confirmed your cell number, ma'am. Thank you."

"What do we do with Adam next?" Diana asked the physician and the deputy. The deputy answered first, "Well, we've found no outstanding arrest warrants—he's committed no crime, and he's not under arrest. So I'm going home. I'll be in touch if we need anything else. Thank you, Ms. Norris."

"Thank you, officer," Dr. Bailey said. After the deputy left, Dr. Bailey said, "Ms. Norris, do you know if Adam has any family in Dallas—or otherwise?"

"Both of his parents are deceased. He has never spoken to me of siblings or any other family. He may have been married and divorced, but I'm not positive—and I've no idea where his ex-wife may live. Sorry. I'm probably the closest thing he has to family in Texas."

"Medically, my best guess is that he is suffering from retrograde amnesia. We found no head trauma. We cannot predict how long his amnesia will last. We expect that one day, something will click, and some or all of his memory will return. But we could be wrong; it may never return. Today might really be the first day of the rest of his life.

"He cannot tell us where he works or where he lives. He doesn't recall for sure if he's married, but he said maybe. He cannot tell us if he ever used recreational drugs, but he does seem to recognize the name Caroline Norris. How long have Adam and Caroline been engaged?"

"Just a couple of weeks, maybe three weeks."

"Where were they going?"

"I don't know. They said they'd tell me when they got back. I know Caroline wanted to go to Aruba."

"Do you know if he was taking any medicines?"

"Just dietary supplements like fish oil and vitamin pills. I've never seen him take any prescription medications. I could look in his home. Dr. Bailey, you said that you had some unanswered questions. Can you tell me what the biggest riddle is?"

"Ms. Norris, we really have only one big unanswered question. As I told you, we cannot explain how anyone could have been on that plane when it crashed and survive—let alone escape without so much as a scratch. We have no rational explanation. Frankly, we keep thinking we'll find that he fooled everyone. Right now, we're skeptical that he was on board that plane.

"If you're able, you should probably keep an eye on him for a few days. We asked him to stay here for observation for a couple of days, but he insists on leaving. So he's hoping to leave here with you. Can you take him home?"

"Yes. I will. He's one of my closest friends. I'll try to help him discover his past too."

"Good. I hope you'll encourage him to see me regularly in my Dallas office—I gave him my card. Here's my card. Call me if you need to.

"Remember. He's not retarded. He lacks confidence because he knows he cannot remember his own past—so he may be socially awkward, since he does not know who he is yet. Be patient."

She said, "Thank you. I will." But she thought, *What the Hell am I getting myself into?*

Chapter 2: The Trip Home

Diana's cell phone rang, and she answered it by saying, "Hi, Skip. No, he's with me and we're on our way back to Plano. Amnesia, nothing else. Just a minute, I'll ask him." She put the phone in her lap, and she looked at Adam, "D'you want to talk with Skip on the phone?"

"Who's Skip? Doesn't matter. No, I don't feel like talking with anyone. Maybe tomorrow. Sorry."

"Adam is not really up to talking right now, Skip. You probably should wait at least two or three days. He doesn't remember me, he doesn't remember you. The doctor in Waco said that he probably has retrograde amnesia. We don't know how long it'll take for him to regain his memory. Yes, I'll tell him. Thanks for calling."

Diana broke the silence as she drove them north toward Dallas on Interstate 35. "I'm going to listen to some music to calm my nerves, Adam. I'll keep it low so we can talk if you want to. Is that okay?"

"Sure. Fine." Adam really could not think of anything to say to her, because in his mind, she was a total stranger, he was still in shock, and he was on a medication Dr. Bailey had given him.

"Is there any kind of music you want to listen to?"

"No thanks."

They had not driven far when Diana became dissatisfied with the songs the satellite radio stations were playing, so she put a CD in the radio/CD player. Adam said, "I like their sound. Who is it?"

"Alison Krauss and Union Station. You and Caroline liked them and went to their concert a few months ago."

Adam was silent but not sullen as Diana drove them back to the Metroplex. He stared at the geodesic dome church on the east side of the Interstate in Waxahachie and thought, *I think I've seen that church before. Maybe I should ask Diana.* But he didn't.

He listened closely to the last song on the CD and said, "Can we listen to that song again? I didn't understand all the words."

"Sure. The title is 'There Is A Reason.' Do you like it?"

"I like the overall sound. I'm not sure what the lyrics are saying. Maybe." Twice Adam asked Diana to play that song again. She tried to help him understand all the words, but she was not completely successful.

"Tomorrow, or another day soon, if you remind me, I'll see if I can find the lyrics to this song on the Internet for you, so you can read them. What is it that caught your attention?"

"Is she singing something about Jesus?"

Diana's voice betrayed some mild surprise as she said, "I think so. That's what it sounds like to me. Why d'you ask?"

"I just find it interesting, that's all. Thanks. He thought, *Is God still trying to say something to me?*"

Long periods of silence were broken by short periods of conversation. The Sirius XM satellite radio was on station 76, the Symphony Hall, but the volume was low and coming only from the rear speaker, so conversation was not prevented, and silent pauses were not overly awkward.

"Thank you for helping me, Diana."

"If you hadn't lost your memory, you'd know that you're like a cross between an uncle and a big brother to me—and you'd not be surprised by my help."

"How do you know me? Are we related?"

"You may not remember me, but we are very close. I told you, I'm Caroline's sister, Diana. You and she were engaged. What do you remember? Do you remember anything about Caroline?"

"I think so. Maybe a little. Did she have red hair?'

"Yes. Red-blonde hair."

"I think I remember that. And she was a couple of inches shorter than you?"

"No. Taller, not shorter."

"That's what I said. Was she a nurse?"

"Yes, she was a nurse."

"I think I remember that. Did we have any children?"

"No."

"Still good. Did she ride a motorcycle? A black Harley?"

"Yes and no. A dark blue Harley. I can't decide if I should sell it or ride it. What d'you think?"

"I think....uh... I think....Well, I think I remember the bike. Do the two of you share an apartment?"

"Yes."

"That's about all I remember—except, for some reason, I think I was hopelessly in love with her."

"Right again. You were."

For a time, they rode in silence, and then somewhere near Duncanville, Adam shut the radio off and asked, "Diana, do you know me well enough to tell me what kind of a person I am?"

"What do you mean? How many kinds are there? You're a good, hardworking, generous, and compassionate man." He was happy to hear that his closest friends considered him good.

"Tell me anything you know about me, Diana. Just don't exaggerate. If I'm a jerk, tell me. And tell me about Caroline and me. What was our relationship like?"

"Like most people, you can be a jerk at times. But most often I think you're the kindest and gentlest man I've ever known. Caroline said you were the most considerate person she'd ever met. She adored you, but you two did have a few fights."

"What'd we argue about?"

"Oh, different things. Once it was about money. Once it was about a guy I was dating. She always complained about your driving—Caroline always thought you drove too aggressively and too fast. Your driving in Dallas traffic made her nervous and tense. She wished you'd stop riding a motorcycle—at least in the city. Caroline had regular bouts with PMS, and you were not very empathetic then. You would just stay away from her until she wasn't so cranky."

"That's not too good. Where do my parents live?"

"They lived in southern Alabama—not far from the Florida panhandle in Gordon, near Dothan.

"Lived? Past tense? Where do they live now?"

"You told us that they died in a car accident when you were a senior at UT in Austin."

"Oh."

After another pause, she continued, "You were very generous to me, Adam. I always thought you must be very wealthy. You paid off my biggest school loan. And once you gave me a hundred dollar bill as I was going out on a date with a guy who you said was a jackass. You told me not to spend it unless I had a major emergency. You called it *mad money*. I still have it in my purse. I never got that mad on a date. D'you need it back?"

"No. Keep it. You still may need it."

"Oh, this car we're in? You bought it for me a few months ago. In one three-week period, I spent over four hundred dollars in repairs on my old car—my only ride to school and to work. A month later, it needed major engine repairs and four new tires. I asked you for advice. All you said was 'You must have dependable transportation for school and for work, but you should postpone a decision until Tuesday. Until then, ride the bus.' Your 'ride-the-bus' suggestion infuriated me."

"So what happened?"

"You really don't remember? Okay, I rode the bus for a few days. On the Monday evening before that Tuesday, you brought a large pizza—pepperoni and Italian sausage—a six pack of beer for you and a bottle of wine for me and Caroline—over to our apartment. After we ate, you asked to see my car keys. When I gave them to you, you handed me a different set of keys and said, 'Let's go see your new car and take it out for a spin.' You'd bought a year-old, low-mileage program car with a great maintenance record, satellite radio, and OnStar. The tires had more than half their life expectancy left—the car looked brand new. It was titled in my name and insured for six months. You even filled the gas tank! Caroline never told me if she was in on the surprise. Did she help pay for my car?"

"Girl, do you remember? I have amnesia?"

"And you don't remember? Very convenient. Well, don't worry—I'm sure your memory will return in a few days—with my help."

"What d'you do, Diana?"

"I'm in graduate school at UT Dallas, and I work part-time as a paralegal."

"Do you earn enough to pay the monthly rent and utilities?"

"I don't know yet. I may have to quit school and get a full time job or find a cheaper apartment. Caroline was subsidizing my education."

"How old are you?"

"Just 26 and completely unattached." Diana said this only because it was her spontaneous, oft-repeated reply to any question about her personal life, but it made Adam wonder.

They first went to Adam's condo—Diana had a key. She led him to the door and stepped aside as he unlocked it. He walked around his condominium trying to find anything he might recognize. She looked in the bathroom cabinets and found no medicines and made a mental note to tell Dr. Bailey.

He picked up a framed picture of Caroline, and asked, "Who's this? Do I have a sister? Is this Caroline?"

"Yes. That's Caroline, your late fiancée."

"She looks different. Is that a good picture of her?"

"It is. She cut her hair at the beginning of summer."

"I think I remember her with longer hair. Who's the man?"

Before Diana could say, "You," Adam chortled and blurted out, "That's me! I didn't recognize me in this picture at first. And Caroline doesn't look exactly like I remember her. Where was this taken, and how long ago?"

"Last summer, we were sailing at Lake Ray Hubbard, on your catamaran. You're right. Her hair was longer then—she cut it a few weeks later—and you said that you liked it shorter too."

Diana showed him an older picture when Caroline's hair was longer. "That's the way I remember her. How much older was I than Caroline? I look much older in this picture."

"Just three years. Most people said she looked younger than her age."

"Was Caroline ever married?"

"No. She was engaged a couple of times before she met you."

"Where'd she work?"

"She was an ER nurse at UT Southwestern Hospital—and loved it. She said it was exciting."

Nothing else in the condo caught his attention. Nothing sparked memories of her. He looked through his clothes closet and thought, *all the clothes in this closet look drab—monotonously boring. I must get some color.* "These are the clothes I usually wore?"

"Yes. Navy blue, black, gray, or khaki Dockers, button-up shirt, and a matching sports coat or seasonal sweater. You were always well-groomed, fashionable, and stylish—even at a picnic. You almost never wore a tie. The only times we ever saw you in anything else was if you two went to the rodeo or line dancing with Caroline—and you wore cowboy boots, Levis, and a cowboy shirt—or went to the pool and wore swim trunks.

"Do you know how old you are, Adam?"

Adam was thinking, *I went dancing? What's 'line dancing'?* "I saw my birthdate on my driver's license and calculated that I'm about 30."

"Close. 29. In four months you have a birthday and turn 30. Your birthday is a few weeks before Caroline's. I need to get home. Are you okay to stay here by yourself tonight?"

"Not really, but I guess I'll figure it out. This whole amnesia thing is scary. I'm nervous. But I cannot think of a better alternative than staying here. I'm sure I'll probably be okay."

"You could stay in Caroline's room for a few days—if that wouldn't be too weird or stressful for you."

"I'm not sure. But I don't want to be alone with myself. Are you sure that I wouldn't be intruding on you?"

"Not at all. I'll enjoy the company. It's close—about a five-minute-drive from here. Come on." After she parked the car, Adam followed her into her apartment.

Diana said, "Make yourself comfortable. D'you want a drink?"

"Sure. What do I drink?"

"Usually a Tom Collins or a Screwdriver."

"I'll try a Tom Collins. Thanks."

A moment later, Diana handed him his drink, but after one taste, he abandoned it. With a twisted face, he said, "Goodness. I used to like that? What's in it? Kerosene? It tastes like shoe polish."

"Hey, that used to be one of your favorite expressions. It has lemon juice, club soda, Gibley's gin. When did you taste shoe polish? Was it Shinola?"

He ignored her teasing and asked, "What are you drinking? May I taste it?"

"A martini. Sure. Here."

"That's not much better. What was Caroline's favorite drink?"

"She hardly ever drank alcohol. She liked real lemonade or root beer. When she drank mixed drinks, it was usually a Bloody Mary or Margarita."

"Next time, I'll try one of those, please. What's in a Screwdriver?"

"Orange juice and vodka."

"I think I like orange juice. Do I drink beer?"

"Some, not much. You like lager much more than ale. But you claim that both have too many calories. You have some beer in the refrigerator. Want one?"

"Yes, please."

"Glass or can?"

"Whatever I usually take, thanks."

A moment later, she handed him a Pilsner glass, full and topped with a foam head. He mumbled an obligatory "Thank you." Adam made no comment about the taste of beer, but the way he drank the whole thing, Diana assumed he was very thirsty or beer was more to his liking.

"I'm going to watch yesterday's episode of 'Jeopardy.' I record it every day. Do you want to watch it with me? Caroline and you often watched it with me. It might trigger a memory."

"Sure. Okay." They sat at opposite ends of a sofa, and Diana noticed that Adam answered none of the items—quite the opposite of his past habit. No new memories appeared, and Adam's interest in the game show quickly waned. Diana noticed his lack of interest and shut the TV off.

Adam began talking in a low voice, as if he were speaking confidentially. "Diana, I won't tell you the whole story tonight—and probably not even this week. But I want to ask you some questions about me and hope you'll be completely candid about who I am, or who I was."

"I can do that."

"Was I a Republican, or a Democrat?"

"Neither. Nor an Independent. Privately you called them all," she lowered her voice to sound like a man, "'Day-Yim lying bastards' and wished you could vote them all out of office. You said it privately so as not to offend potential clients."

"I had clients? What kind of clients?"

"Real estate, you worked at Terry Realtors. I've already called them. They're not expecting to see you until the Monday or Tuesday after Caroline's funeral."

Diana was thankful that their conversation stopped for a few minutes. Then Adam continued, "Was I very religious?"

"You? Religious?" She laughed, "Hell no! Heavens no! To close friends, you claimed to be an atheist. To acquaintances who were religious, you said you were agnostic-but-open. To strangers, you said you were 'very spiritual' but not very religious, and declined to expand on that description. Why do you ask that?"

"Because I have magnesia. For..."

"Amnesia, not magnesia."

"Whatever, I keep forgetting. For some reason, I guessed I was an atheist, but I wasn't sure." After a pause, he continued. "Diana, where'd you and Caroline go to church?"

"St. Andrew's on 15th St.—when we went, which wasn't very often. Just twice a year: Christmas Eve and Good Friday or Easter Sunday. You went with us once, Adam. We liked it. You said it was too liturgical—we weren't sure what you meant, but we could tell you didn't intend it as a compliment."

"Do you know if my parents took me to church as a kid?"

"I don't think so. But you told us that your maternal grandparents did. I think they were Methodist or Baptist and attended whichever church was closest to their home. Why?"

"Diana, do you know God?"

"Totally. I went to parochial school, so sure. What d'you want to know about God?"

"I'm not asking you if you know *about God.* I'm asking if *you know God.*"

"Oh. I'm not really sure anyone can know God. Why do you ask?"

"I'll probably tell you sometime, but not tonight. I'm too tired and too confused right now. Don't let me wear out my welcome, Diana. When you get tired of my hanging out with you, tell me. Promise?"

"Sure. I promise." *As if that will ever happen,* she thought. "The church Caroline and I went to as kids taught that the Bible is the best revelation of God."

"Do you personally believe that too?"

"Yes, I do. And spare me your cries of 'delusion'!"

"Okay. Do you really believe that the Bible is the best revelation of God?"

"I do."

"How often do you read the Bible? Do you also read books about interpreting it?"

Diana thought for a moment, caught off-guard by the intensity of Adam's questions. "I read it when I think I need it, I guess, and I don't recall ever reading a book about the Bible—except maybe as a student in parochial school."

"If you really believe that the Bible is the best revelation of God, why aren't you reading and studying it every day so you can know God?"

"Because I...well, of course, people, uh, don't always...damn, Adam. I don't know. But I know that I believe in God!"

"What do you mean, 'I believe in God'? Do you just mean that you believe God exists? Or something else?"

Diana laughed as she said, "Oh, no. I'm not going to answer any more of your trick God-questions just so you can attack my answers! Adam, you don't even believe in God—you're a damned atheist! Where are you going with all these God-questions?"

"I don't know. I don't even know myself—there's no way I could know God. I don't even know you."

Diana paused and then spoke very quietly with a measured cadence, "Yes you do, Adam. You are my best friend—well, my best male friend. Please don't be mad at me."

"I'm not mad at you, child. I'm frustrated with myself."

Diana shouted, "Dammit, Adam, don't you ever call me 'child' again!" Her angry outburst startled him.

Adam hugged Diana as most guys would hug a younger sister. She did not return his hug but let her arms hang limp at her sides as Adam said, "Seriously, I'm sorry. I meant that in an affectionate way, Kiddo. I didn't mean to insult you." After a moment, he released her and the tension slowly subsided.

With a nostalgic tone, she said, "You always used to call me Kiddo." Then her voice changed. "Come on." Diana led him to Caroline's bedroom door, "This is the master bedroom with an attached full bathroom. You spent many nights here. Make yourself at home." By this time she was no longer emotional.

When Diana left the room, Adam scrutinized every detail of Caroline's room hoping something would trigger more memories—but no luck. The décor was decidedly feminine—attractively, not excessively. Adam thought, *Caroline must have had an artistic flair.* The queen-size bed smelled like a bouquet of flowers, but the aroma was not overpowering. *I know that aroma!* It seemed sensual and almost sparked a romantic memory—but he was unsure of himself—so he called to Diana, who was still up watching her game show on TV.

"Diana, did I sleep here recently?"

His question, tone of voice, and facial expression made her suspect that Adam's memory was being restored. "Yes. The night before the crash. Why? Do you remember something?"

"Was I alone? Or did Caroline sleep here too?"

"She was with you. Do you have a restored memory?"

"Almost. Maybe." *Can a person almost remember something? Probably not.* "I'm going to try to go to sleep now. G'night."

"I hope you sleep well, Adam. G'night."

About 1:00 A.M., Adam awakened and heard a noise in the next room. At first he was unsure what it was, but he finally recognized it as sobbing. He very quietly slipped out of bed and into his pants, walked to the door, and opened it a few inches. In the darkness he could barely see Diana seated on floor, but he could not see what she was doing. She was seated with her back to him, so her body was between him and whatever she was working with. Twice he heard her say, "Damn." He heard clicking sounds of metal hitting metal. He thought, *Does she have knives? I sure hope she doesn't have knives.*

He was thankful that the carpeted floor muffled any sound of him walking toward her. He found a light switch and raised it. The light startled Diana, who flopped on the floor prostrate and crying, "I cannot figure out how to load the damn thing. I cannot even kill myself. I'm such a failure!"

Adam quickly moved to separate the gun and ammunition some distance from Diana. Adam did not recall that he had given the sisters a pink Taurus .32 caliber semiautomatic handgun for Christmas a couple of years ago. He and Caroline would occasionally go shoot at a gun range, but Diana had never earned a Concealed Handgun License or fired the gun..

He said, "Diana, what the Hay-Yil are you doing?" But he was thinking, *Should I call 911? Should I have her admitted for observation?*

She was so hysterical, he could hardly understand her, "I've no reason to live. I just want to die. Help me, Adam. I couldn't find any pills to take to end my life, and I didn't have the courage to use a razor blade. So I tried to use the gun. But I couldn't to load it."

"Diana, think of how your death would affect the people who know and love you! Didn't parochial school teach you that a person who kills herself goes straight to Hell?"

"Yeah, they taught me that, but I never believed them. After a day of mourning, no one would miss me. The only person who ever really loved me is gone. I have no reason to live. I just want to die—painlessly."

"Here, put your robe on." While she was doing that, he retrieved a pillow from her bed, sat on the sofa, and put the pillow in his lap. "Come lie down on the sofa, Diana, put your head on the pillow in my lap and talk to me." She was in no hurry, but she did as she was told. "Now breathe deeply and tell me all your feelings."

Through her more composed grief she said, "Caroline has been part of my life since the day I was born. We have photos of her giving me a bath when I was a baby, holding my hands as she taught me to walk. I never went to kindergarten, because Caroline taught me letters and numbers. All through school she helped me with my homework—even math!" All of this spilled out of Diana in a torrent, and then her emotions took over, "And now she's gone, gone forever. No one will ever love me as she loved me—even when I was a brat she loved me. Adam you are the closest friend I have. Please, don't ever leave me."

"You know I won't. I cannot become Caroline, but I'll always be your friend."

"Promise?"

"Yes, I promise."

She lay with her head on the pillow in his lap, and in a few minutes she was dozing off, but Adam was asking himself questions. *Do I take the gun to my home? Do I help her get psychiatric counseling? Maybe I'll ask her to go see Dr. Bailey with me in a few days.* He waited about fifteen more minutes before he carried her into her bedroom and gently put her in her bed. *I'm glad she isn't any heavier.* Then he went in Caroline's bedroom, closed and locked the door, and hid the gun between the mattress and the box spring.

That night the strange dream that had been disturbing Adam returned. It seemed so real, that it took him several minutes the next morning to realize it was just a dream.

At dawn the next day, as Adam drifted toward consciousness, even before he opened his eyes, he remembered that he was in Caroline's bed and bedroom. As he lay on his right side, he opened and closed his eyes a few times, taking stock of where he was. He knew something was not right, but he could not identify what. Since he could see both of his hands in front of his face, he was startled to feel something move on his bare waist. *What the…. Is that a hand?* He very slowly rolled over on his back and then his left side and was shocked to find Diana lying beside him in bed—apparently still asleep. *Where did she come from? I thought I locked the door—how did she get in?*

Adam moved as far as he could to the side of the bed away from Diana. *How did she get into bed with me without waking me up? When did she get in bed with me?* His movement awakened her, and they stared at each other, not knowing what to say.

Diana closed her eyes and said, "Adam, I'm sorry. A dream awakened me around 4:00 A.M. In the dream, Caroline called for me to come be with her. When I was fully awake, I realized that it was a dream, and then I remembered what I tried to do last night. The dream seemed so real, it took me a while to realize it was just a dream. Fear paralyzed me and grief over Caroline overwhelmed me.

"After crying for a while, I opened your door to see if you were alright. I couldn't bear being alone. So I slipped into bed beside you. I wasn't trying to…uh, to…my actions were totally innocent and pure—I promise you." Diana opened her eyes and glanced at Adam, and then she looked away.

Adam said, "Diana, I'm so confused, and this only bewilders me more. You're certainly attractive and physically desirable, but I do not know who I am. And the Adam you knew may have died with Caroline in the plane crash. Please assure me that this will never happen again. I desperately need emotional stability right now. My whole world is chaotic! I really want to be a close friend, but we cannot become sexually intimate. I cannot—I must not—take advantage of you."

"And I must not take advantage of you. I'm so embarrassed and sorry, Adam…" she began, but tears ended her apology. Adam wanted to hold her and reassure her. He thought, *that'll definitely have to wait until we're both fully dressed and not in bed together!*

"Diana, did Caroline and I have a sexual relationship? Did we sleep together?"

"If you two ever slept, it was the noisiest sleeping in human history."

"And, what about you and me? Diana, did we ever…?"

"Gosh no, never. You were completely focused on Caroline. You idolized her."

Finally he broke the tension by saying, "Hey! In that case, it's all good, Diana. Get up. Let's go get some breakfast, take a long walk in the park, and talk about how you can help me discover who I was, and then I'll try to discover who I will be." She kept her robe tight around her as she left the room and said, "You use the shower in there, and I'll use the other shower. The last one ready to go buys breakfast."

He shouted, "Agreed," but he moved slowly to make sure he lost.

Fifteen minutes later Diana was behind the wheel, and they were driving off to find breakfast. As they sat and ate their food at McDonald's, Diana asked him, "Why were you asking me about God last night, Adam? Are you still a convinced atheist? Have you become a believer, or what?"

"I don't know. I think I need to first discover what I was, and then try to figure out what I believe now. But I don't know how to do either one.

"I looked on the Internet and found several hundred churches, synagogues, mosques, and other places of worship in the D/FW area. Exploring all these churches would literally take years! Religion is pretty complex and chaotic.

"Does God care what I believe, say, do, or don't do? Does it matter if I go to church? Does God care where I go to church? I don't know God—but, if God exists, I'd like to know that he exists. And I think I'd like to know him.

"So I guess I'm on a quest to know God—at least to know if he exists. What do you think, Diana? Does God exist? If so, which god?"

"I was raised Protestant and went to parochial school, so of course I believe that God exists. But I don't know how to help you here. I guess you need to talk to a priest or a minister. But if God exists—the one they taught me about in school—he should be able to reveal himself to you without help from a priest, minister, or church."

"Yeah. Really. Good point. I think I'm going to visit a few churches, but I don't know which ones."

"Then maybe God could directly guide you—or provide a human friend to guide you to him."

Adam said, "If he can't, he cannot really be God, can he?" He thought, *at least not the God who rescued me from the airplane!*

With no context to help Adam interpret her meaning, Diana said, "If you want me to, Adam, I could dye my hair red."

"Why would you think I'd like that? Why do you suggest that?"

"Everyone said Caroline and I almost looked like twins—except for the hair color."

"Oh, Diana, nothing will ever replace Caroline—nobody. No, don't do that. You don't really look that much like her anyway. And your jet-black hair is just as dramatically attractive as her red hair was."

"You think so?"

"You favor her, Diana, but you're even better looking. You have a cuter nose and a better figure."

Diana loved flattery. "Awww, thanks, Adam. You make me blush. Tell me more."

Now he was smiling. "Well, she was smarter and more mature—more stable and more sentimental. She was an inch or two taller. She was very comfortable with herself, more self-confident than you are. And much less obnoxiously flirtatious and narcissistic."

"Hey, I'm sitting right here," she said as she laughed and flirtatiously slapped him on the arm.

"Oh, sorry. I didn't see you there. What do you see as the major personality difference between you and Caroline?"

"She was more feminine—well, that's not the right word really. She was a frilly-girl, a 'girly-girl.' I've got a little bit more of the 'tom-boy' in me than she had. I enjoy tent camping and fishing, and she couldn't put bait on a hook or take a fish off the hook. Her idea of roughing it was staying in an inexpensive motel. I went hunting with Dad a couple of times, and helped clean rabbits, squirrels, and once, a deer.

"She never went fishing or hunting with Dad. She never helped him clean fish or butcher a deer. She was always afraid she'd break a nail or mess up her hair. I just wanted to be with my dad and do things with him. She was more conscious of fashion—and much more artistic, so she was my unpaid volunteer fashion advisor, criticizing what I wore each day.

"Adam, you like to camp, too. You like to camp places where you can also hike and canoe. Maybe we'll go camping sometime. Caroline was never interested in camping."

"Where do you like to camp?"

"New Mexico, Louisiana, Colorado, Tennessee, North Carolina, Florida, and…."

He interrupted, "Where near Texas—within 100 miles of north Dallas?"

"Hmmm, Lake Murray State Park near Ardmore, Oklahoma, and almost any of the parks on Lake Texoma."

"Maybe one day we'll go camping. First I have to sort out my life."

"I'll hold you to that promise."

"I said *maybe*—saying maybe does not constitute a promise."

"I heard a promise, and that's all that counts."

He thought, *I don't like it when you use your beauty and charms to manipulate me. Caroline never did that. How can I help you learn not to do that without hurting you, Kiddo?*

Chapter 3: Back Home

"Diana, can you take me to my condo again sometime today?" The question did not surprise her, because Adam had avoided driving since the plane crash.

"Yes. I have one class today, and I'll be back around nine-thirty—we can go then if that's early enough."

"That's fine. I'll just hang here and search the Internet while you're gone, but you'll have to get the computer connected online before you leave."

About nine-fifty they arrived at Adam's condo. "What are you looking for, Adam?"

"Any clues about me, about who I was."

"Well, you have lots of books. Biographies, fiction, nonfiction, historical fiction Civil War, World War I and II. Did you ever read them? Or were they just for show?"

"I've no idea."

"Here's an anthology by Zenna Henderson. *Ingathering: The Complete People Stories of Zenna Henderson.* And several books by Robert Heinlein. I didn't know that you liked science fiction."

She chuckled when he said, "I didn't know that either."

"Well, you might try reading one of them and see if you can remember any of the storyline. Adam, all I see in your refrigerator is beer and cheese. And I don't think this oven has ever been used—it looks brand new. Did you ever cook or eat here?"

Instead of answering her question, he said, "Hey, look at all these keys! Wow! I wonder what they unlock."

Diana took them from his hand and said, "This one is for your Mercedes-Benz SL. This one is for your Ford Edge SE. This one goes with your restored 1950 GMC pickup truck. This one is for the lock on the door of your condo. You don't keep your Harley key on this key ring. I don't know what the other keys fit—probably they're keys for locks at work."

"I guess the computer is mine, but I don't remember how to turn it on or run it."

"I'll boot it up for you."

In a couple of minutes she said, "It's protected with a password."

"Sorry. I don't have a clue what the password is. Now what do we do?"

"Hhmmm. If you were creating a password right now, what would it be?"

"Nothing is coming to my mind."

"Let me try caroline.

"No, not lowercase caroline, maybe with a capital C.

"That didn't work either. "I'll try 'carolinenorris, all lowercase—nope, still no good.

"Let me capitalize the C and the N."

Adam said, "Wait a minute! Try Caroline Anne Norris as one word, all lowercase except with a capital C, A, and N."

"Okay. Just a sec, hit enter, wait…it's thinking, and Bingo-Dingo! That's it! You're amazing, Adam! Did you remember that?"

"I'm not sure, maybe. I'll play with the computer later. I'm checking mail now." Adam sat at his desk and rummaged through a short stack of old mail. "I was a member of the American Humanist Association. I guess that's good. I'm an American, and I think I'm human. Aren't I?"

"Some of your friends might debate that, but, yeah, I think you are. You have lots of back issues of *The Humanist*—their magazine. You once told me that the only groups you joined were the AHA, the National Association of Realtors, and a motorcycle rider's club. You often told me that you were not a 'joiner.' But I think you were also a member of the National Rifle Association."

"Well, that's good news, I guess. Hey, here's a letter I was writing to Henry. Apparently he's my cousin—unless I was in the habit of calling all of my friends 'cousin.' The whole letter attacks his religion. Why would I give a She-Yit if someone's religious? We live in the home of the free—or is it the home of the brave?"

"Both. You were the 'Apostle of Atheism.' I think it started when your parents died together in a car accident and maybe a reaction to your grandmother's harsh religion." *And*, she thought, *the death of your baby boy.*

Adam abruptly said, "Shh! Listen!" Adam put a forefinger in front of his pursed lips, signaling 'be quiet.'

Diana whispered, "What is it?"

He pointed and said, "Someone's at the front door."

They stood by the door as it opened. A short, stout Latina walked in, saw them, and threw up her hands screaming, "Aaahhhhh! *Dios me protege!* Senõr Bowers! You scared me to death. What's the matter with you? I was so close to death, I'm sure I heard the angels in Heaven singing."

It took a moment for the commotion to morph to laughter. Adam used a matter-of-fact tone of voice when he said, "I was in an accident and have a memory problem. Who are you, and where did you get a key to my home?"

"Oh, you know me, Senõr Bowers, I'm Maria. I clean your home from top to bottom every week. I feel dizzy—oh, maybe I should sit down for a minute." Adam and Diana steadied her as she sat on the nearest chair.

Diana was still laughing as she said, "Hi, Maria. I'm Diana Norris. I'm sorry we startled you. *Que Dios te dé su paz.* May I get you some water or something else to drink?'

'No thank you.'

'You do an excellent job of cleaning Adam's condo. He's not a neatnik, and the condo is very neat and clean—thanks to you, I'm sure."

"*Gracias*, Diana. He is here almost never when I clean. I think my heart it stopped, and now it's still not running right even."

"Adam has amnesia, Maria. He remembers almost nothing of his past."

"Oh, I am so sorry, Senõr Bowers." Maria had an empathetic facial expression. "In that case, I will help. You always leave a check in an envelope on the mantle for me so you don't have to buy a stamp and mail me a check."

"Did you hear that, Adam? You're too cheap to buy a stamp. Cheapskate."

"Not cheap—frugal. Yeah. I found my checkbook in the desk a few minutes ago. I'll go write her a check now." In a few minutes, he found a check stub and called, "Maria, is your last name Garcia?"

"Si. *Mi nombre es García*, Senõr Bowers."

"And I pay you fifty dollars? Every week?"

"Si, every week. Today, one hundred fifty dollars! On my way home I'll go to Urgent Care—for my heart attack!" They all laughed at her tease.

And even though Adam knew she was joking, he wrote the check for that amount—with Diana's help. *I hope I was always generous.*

Maria showed them a safe in the closet off of the master bedroom, but she had no idea what the combination was. Adam could not recall the combination to the safe or what was in it. Diana said she'd contact the manufacturer next week to see how to solve that problem.

Then she went to the computer and opened Windows File Explorer and searched for a file named passwords. She found no file with that name, but she found a folder named password and opened it and found a DOC file named *keys*. She could not open it—it too was password protected. 'Caroline,' Carol,' and 'CarolineAnnNorris' all failed as passwords too. "Adam, when you were a child, did you have a dog or a cat?"

"How would I know? Diana, I don't remember anything—I have ambrosia."

"Amnesia, not ambrosia. Right. Sorry. So if you were making up a password right now, what would you use?"

Adam looked over her shoulder at his computer and said, "Toshiba, capital T. What's ambrosia?"

"It's a fruit salad that's fit for the Greek pantheon."

In a few seconds, the *keys* file opened, and Diana wrote down the combination to the safe.

"Go with me right now to the racetrack and pick a horse, Adam. I'll invest some cash in the horse you pick. You must be the luckiest person in the world—today, anyway!"

They opened the safe together and inventoried the contents, putting each of them on a nearby table. Diana listed the contents on a pad of paper.

Adam said, "Handgun and ammunition. Glock, model LMS-1131P. Two boxes of 9mm cartridges, fifty rounds in each."

Diana replied, "Check, check." And this continued.

"Deeds, stocks, incorporation papers, and other legal documents."

"Check, check, check, check."

"Some letters." Diana noticed two envelopes with return addresses for attorneys.

"Check. Adam, is TR being sued?" His look reminded her, "Ooops. I know, you have ambrosia. Sorry."

Adam said, "Some coins and jewelry—half a dozen diamonds" and put that on the table.

"Check."

"A peculiar looking key."

"Let me see. That could be a key to a safe deposit drawer at a bank. See, it's stamped DO NOT DUPLICATE. When you go back to work, someone there will probably know what it's for."

Then Adam said, "Here's a shoebox on the bottom shelf." He looked in it, but he immediately put it back in the safe and said, "More legal papers and letters. That's all."

But the way he said it made her suspicious. "Don't you want to put it on the table too? Then I can wipe the dust off the shelves with a cloth before we lock them back up."

"No. I didn't see much dust anyway." He started putting things back in the safe.

When the last item was in the safe, he closed the door and locked it.

"Let's look at my old photo albums now. Maybe it'll jog my memory."

"Okay."

After looking through seven or eight of the albums, Diana selected a few albums to take to her apartment. Later she and Adam looked through them. Diana could identify a few of the people, but many of them would remain unknown unless Adam's memory returned. Even later, after Adam learned to name people in the family pictures, at times he was unsure that he remembered someone from the past, or just remembered that Diana had told him who was in the picture.

During one of the sessions looking at family pictures, Adam said, "Diana, I've changed my mind. I'm not going to look at any more pictures of family or friends for a while."

"What? Why Adam? Don't you think one of these might trigger your memory?"

"I'm not sure, but it hasn't worked yet. Here's what I fear could happen: You've shown me pictures of my parents and my dog, Prince. In the future, as I try to prove to myself and others that I'm regaining my memory, I may deceive myself. I might see a picture and say, 'That's my dog, Prince' or 'That's a picture of my parents.' And really, all I'm doing is remembering that sometime after the plane crash, someone told me that these were my parents or my dog. Do you see?

"Without ever seeing these pictures since the crash and having someone tell me who they are, one day I will say to you or someone, 'Get the photo album with the floral cover, look toward the front—maybe the third or fourth page—on the top right, there's a picture of my mother with her sister, my Aunt Virginia in a red blouse, and her four children, my cousins.' You'll open that album and find that picture. And when I can do that repeatedly, you'll say, 'Adam, you've regained your memory.' And I'll say, 'Yes ma'am.'

"I need to be able to trust my memory again."

In about three hours, Maria finished cleaning and departed. Then Adam and Diana went to a nearby Panera Bread. As they sat at a table washing down chicken salad sandwiches with sweet iced tea, Diana said, "Oh, my gosh! Don't turn around Adam. There's Juan!"

He looked over his shoulder and said, "Juan who? Who's Juan?" But his voice lacked the emotion in Diana's voice.

"I said don't look now, Adam! Juan Reyes. He's a guy I dated several months ago. The last time I saw him, we had a terrible argument, and you threw him out of my apartment, telling him to get out and not to come back or call me. You told me to stay away from him."

"Why did I do that? What was your argument with him about?"

"It's not important. Forget it. I don't want to talk about it."

"I want to know. Did he hit you? Or did he 'hit on you'? Or...."

Diana was obviously agitated that Adam insisted on knowing what they fought about. She broke eye contact with Adam by staring at her food as she answered him. "No. If you must know, I invited him to spend the night with me. He wouldn't sleep with me because of his religion. When you heard him trying to tell me about his religion, you became angry and threw him out with much loud profanity. I was so embarrassed. I was scared that you were going to beat the health out of him!"

"Did I hit him?"

"No. Everything but."

"Well, I don't remember any of that. Let's go talk to him. Maybe he can say something that'll restore my memory."

"No. I don't want to see him." Now she looked up at him with pleading eyes. "Please don't, Adam."

"I'm sorry, Diana. If you want to, I'll wait until you leave, then I'll talk to him. You could wait in the car. His name is Juan Reyes?"

"I don't think we should risk it. Besides, he's sitting with a girl."

"Please forgive me, but he might be the key to the restoration of my memory. I cannot miss this possibility."

"Please don't tell him I'm here."

"I won't."

As Adam walked across the room to the table where Juan was seated, Diana moved to a chair that would put her back toward Juan and, she hoped, he would not notice her. Juan looked up to see Adam approaching his table. He took several seconds to connect the approaching man to his memory of Diana.

Juan said, "Please, I don't want any trouble."

Adam stopped and said, "I assure you, Juan, I mean you no harm. Please, just let me talk to you for a moment, and accept my apology for any offense I have ever given you." Juan's face indicated acceptance, but he kept his guard up. "My name is Adam Bowers."

"I know who you are, and I remember what you told me."

Adam continued, "I was in an accident recently and have no memory of our past quarrel. I'm hoping you might be part of my search for my missing memory."

By now, Adam was seated next to the girl at the table, and Juan was a little more relaxed. The girl was nervous, but she did not move. "Adam, this is my fiancée, Esperanza."

"I'm pleased to meet you, Esperanza." He looked back at Juan, "I'm told that you are very religious, Juan. Are you Muslim, Buddhist, Christian, or…?"

"I'm totally committed to Christ Jesus as my Savior and Lord."

"Juan, maybe my meeting you is not an accident. I am on a God–Quest. Maybe you might help me. Where do you go to church?"

"I attend the same Catholic Church I grew up in, and I also worship God at other churches. I'm a Charismatic Catholic." Adam had no idea what that meant. He thought, *I'll ask him about that later, maybe. Getting answers to other questions are more pressing.*

"Juan, do you know God?"

Juan raised his eyebrows and gave him a questioning look. "Yes. I do know God. Why do you ask? Do you know God?"

"No. But I think I've met him—at least once."

"You're not talking about taking hallucinogenic drugs to see God, are you?"

"No, I'm not. I don't know him, but I want to know him. Can you tell me how to know God?"

"I can help you come to know and trust God. But I'm not sure what you have in mind. Is this a trick? The only time we ever met, you told me that you were an atheist, that all religions are false, and that Christians were suffering under a delusion. You threatened me with bodily harm, and I'm really not interested in arguing with you about God. Why should I trust you?"

"I cannot tell you why you should trust me. I have amnesia; I don't know who I was, who I am, or who I'm becoming. All I can tell you now is that I want to find out who God is and what he wants with me. And I will not inflict you with bodily harm."

"God wants something with you? What do you think he wants, Adam?"

"I have no idea."

"Are you romantically involved with Diana?" At first Adam thought of saying, *That's none of your Day-Yim business.* But he recalled he was asking Juan for a favor.

"No. I was engaged to her sister. Caroline was killed a few days ago in a plane crash. I was on that plane too, and I escaped with no injury and almost no memory. There's much more to that story that I'll probably tell you one day, but I won't tell it now. Can I meet God by going to church with you?"

"I'm very sorry to hear about Caroline. Esperanza knew her and told me that she was a very compassionate nurse." Esperanza looked at Adam with a compassionate, empathetic expression on her face. "No, going to church will not make you a Christian. This search venture will probably take time and include several long and deep conversations. Tell me when and where we can meet and get to know each other. We should meet at least once a week. You can tell me what you've experienced and what you believe. And I'll tell you what God has done and is doing in my life." Juan had become bolder as he saw and heard Adam's sincere cry for help and how this meeting had obviously been divinely ordained.

"That sounds reasonable. Do you want to meet here at Panera Bread? I can buy your lunch or dinner. Is Tuesday noon good? Or we can meet at Diana's apart…"

Juan quickly interjected, "No. Here at Panera is better. Every Tuesday is good too. If we meet at lunch, I'd have only twenty minutes before I'd have to return to work. How about 5:30 for dinner? This will give us more time."

"That should be fine, Juan. Thank you for agreeing to help me. I can pay you if you'd like."

"I have already been paid. You should not thank me. You should thank God. His Spirit insists that I help you. Adam, we must pray together before you leave."

Adam looked around the crowded restaurant, hoping no one he knew would see him. He started to say, "Here? People might see us," but Juan had already bowed his head and begun to pray out loud.

"Thank you, Father for your love revealed in Christ Jesus. Thank you for letting me be part of what you're doing in Adam's life. *Gloria a Dios.*" Adam did not realize that Juan was finished praying, since he did not say Amen. Adam never did bow his head or close his eyes, because Adam did not know Juan was praying until he was finished. He thought, *I hope he doesn't have to pray every time he comes to Panera Bread. People will think we're religious fanatics. I sure hope he doesn't bring a Bible with him on Tuesday evenings.*

Juan said, "Adam, let me warn you. If you really want to know God, you cannot be halfhearted in your search. As God told the Jews through the prophet Jeremiah, 'You will seek me and find me when you seek me with all your heart.' I hope you're prepared for the most exciting search of your life.

"And on a more positive note, God also used Jeremiah to tell the Jews 'I will be found by you….'. I have no doubt that God is more eager for you to discover right relationship with him than you are."

Juan and Esperanza stood up to leave. "I'll meet you here this coming Tuesday evening at 5:30, Adam," he said.

"Thanks. I'll be here."

And Esperanza added, "Please ask Diana to come with you. I would like her to come. If she does, I will be here too. If not, I'll let you two men meet without us ladies."

"You should call her and invite her. She'll be more likely to come if you do that, than if I just tell her what you said."

"*Dios te bendiga. Adios.*"

"*Salud. Adios.*"

The men swapped cell phone numbers, and Juan and Esperanza left the restaurant. Adam rejoined Diana and told her of Juan's willingness to help.

Chapter 4: Caroline's Memorial

Five days after the plane crash, Diana and Adam went to a funeral home on West Spring Creek Parkway in Plano to complete plans for Caroline's funeral. Terry Realty had wreaths and signs put on the front and back doors of their offices apologizing and explaining to clients that they were attending a funeral for Caroline Norris. The sign ended by stating, "We plan to be open for business as usual tomorrow." The same message greeted those who called on the business phone.

"Adam, thank you for making all of the funeral arrangements for me."

"You are very welcome, Kiddo. I hope you are okay with the decisions I made, as well." As they approached the funeral home, Adam explained to Diana, "The casket will not be open, because her body was burned almost beyond recognition."

"Good. I'm expecting a large group of ER doctors and nurses dressed in their brightly colored smocks in honor of Caroline. They're planning to sit together at the front of one side of the small chapel. I did not realize how popular Caroline was at Presbyterian Hospital. Did you?"

"Yeah. I did know she was admired, respected, and loved by all her colleagues."

During visitation, the room was crowded with people, flowers, and pictures of Caroline. Some were copies of pictures of her used by her alma mater in student recruitment. Pictures were on the closed casket, on tables, and projected on a large screen.

Later, in the memorial service in the chapel, several people eulogized her. Two of her teachers at nursing school told of her study habits as a student. One said, "Caroline always came to class prepared and asked probing questions. I was careful never to try to teach only half-prepared because her questions would reveal my lack of preparation."

Chiefs of three different departments at Presbyterian Hospital spoke of their experiences with Caroline. The chief of pediatrics—where Caroline worked her first year after finishing nursing school—said, "She was like a big sister to the children in her care. She always gave a child a hug and a present on his or her birthday. She argued that no child should have an operation on his or her birthday—unless his or her life depended on it. This made some nurses think she was superstitious, but she was just being kind. She cried unashamedly whenever one of the children in her care died—and often went to their funerals. She was always upbeat and made optimistic, positive comments. She never saw a child she didn't immediately love."

The Chief of Surgery bragged on her by saying, "Caroline had a unique ability to distract patients and put them at ease before an operation. If she detected anxiety in a patient about to go under the knife, she engaged them in ordinary conversation that focused their thinking on other things. For example, once she asked a nervous patient, 'When you get home and recover, please send me your recipe for pecan pie—especially the crust.' They had a ten minute chat about the best shortening and flour to use and the importance of using cold—but not too cold—water in making pie crust. That lady was still talking pecan pie as the anesthesia put her under. Caroline had switched to banana pudding, but it was too late, the anesthesiologist had already injected Diprivan into her IV. Before she left the hospital, she told Caroline that her friendly, smiling face and their casual conversation about baking a pie eased her mind."

The director of the emergency room told a couple of anecdotes that illustrated her indefatigable optimism and quirky sense of humor. He ended his remarks by saying, "Her death is an enormous loss to our emergency room staff. Caroline was like the glue that held us together—Super Glue." He looked at the closed casket and said, "Good-bye you beautiful super-nurse. You'll be sorely missed." He was so overcome by his emotions during the closing sentence that most people did not know what he said—but they all understood his expression of grief.

Diana was barely able to talk as she tried to eulogize her sister. Her eulogy was very poorly organized, but it came from her distraught heart. "Caroline was my role model. All my life I wanted to be like her. I was crushed when she was angry with me. My big sister made me finish college—and go to graduate school. She always believed in me, helping and encouraging me in anything I did."

Then Diana noticed that Adam was on his feet and approaching the platform. The group guessed he intended to say something. The tension was heightening since virtually everyone present knew he had amnesia, and most did not know that he had some limited memory of Caroline. As he stepped up on the platform, Diana met him and whispered, "Adam, what are you doing?" Those seated on the front rows heard her. Even before the plane crash, Adam could not whisper—everyone in the room heard his reply, "I want to say something too." He sounded a little like a petulant child. Only then did Diana notice that no one had asked Adam if he wanted to eulogize his late fiancée. Instead, they all assumed his amnesia would prevent his participation.

"Of course you can say something, Adam." Diana smiled at the audience, and they smiled back at her. She went to the lectern microphone and said, "Most of you probably know that Caroline and Adam Bowers were engaged to be married in a few months. He survived the crash that took her life. Adam suffers retrograde amnesia, but he remembers a few things about her." By this time Adam was standing next to her, trying to take the microphone, and Diana released her grip on it. It was an awkward, yet poignant, moment.

Adam paused for a moment, looked over the group and said one sentence. "She genuinely loved me." He paused, "And I loved her with…" his voice broke as he said, "all my heart." Then he was overcome with grief and his voice broke as he said the last two or three words. Diana lost control of her emotions, and sobbed hysterically while Adam hugged her, and the small group openly wept with her. For a moment, she seemed to regain her composure and tried to continue eulogizing Caroline, but after a few failed attempts to speak, Adam took her hand and led her back to their seats and sat down next to her. The minister closed that part of the funeral.

They said little during the ride to the cemetery. After the minister finished his graveside remarks, people put flowers on top of the casket in preparation to lower it into the hole in the ground. Diana grabbed Adam by the arm and said, "Make them stop, Adam. I want to open the casket and see her one more time. Make them stop."

"Diana, let her go. We have beautiful pictures and memories. What's in the casket is horrible. We don't want that as our last memory of your sister." She cried in Adam's arms while dirt was thrown on top of the casket. Adam used his body to block her view of the grave and slowly moved Diana further and further away from the hole in the ground. As they walked back to her car, Adam asked, "D'you want me to drive us back home?"

"No, thanks. Give me a minute, I'll be okay. I don't know what came over me."

"It's called grief, Diana, and it'll take some time for you to complete your grief work. It'll come over you when you least expect it. Don't fight it, don't deny it. Just cry—shriek and wail if you feel like it—and never apologize for it. We grieve because we love."

They sat silently in the car for five or six minutes. Finally she started the engine and put it in gear. As she drove back to Plano, Diana asked, "Adam, what did you find most attractive about Caroline?"

"What? Everything. Her face, exquisite; her skin, unblemished; her hair, gorgeous; her feet, delicate. She was the most beautiful person I've ever known. She had it all: looks, character, brains, personality, compassion, humility, artistic talent—she was the complete package. She did not appreciate how physically attractive or smart she was—or if she did, she never acted like it."

"What was the first thing about her that attracted you? Some guys are all about the figure, others notice legs, breasts, or derrière. What do you first notice in a girl that makes you think she's attractive?"

"Her face, followed closely by a cheerful, optimistic personality—if my memory can be trusted here—not to detract from her legs, breasts, or derrière—all of which were beautiful."

Diana said," I think you're remembering more—at least about Caroline!"

"Actually, I read all that in my journal yesterday when we were at my condo."

"Oh. Well, that's nice too I guess. Bring me your journal and I'll proofread it."

"Never."

"Did you ever write anything about me in it?"

"I don't know. I just read a couple of pages—I'd just met Caroline, we'd gone on two or three dates. That part of the journal was written in anticipation of a deeper relationship including...."

"T.D.M.I! T.D.M.I! T.D.M.I!" Diana's boisterous protestation startled Adam.

"What does T.D.M.I. mean?"

"Too Damn Much Information. Stop! I don't want to know anymore."

"Oh, T.D.M.I. I like that. Can I use it? Does everyone know what that means?"

"Everyone who works with me at the law office uses it. Anyone can use it—you don't need to mention my name."

Dusk was falling when they arrived at her apartment, Diana said, "Please, come in and talk to me for a few minutes, Adam."

"Okay."

She adjusted the thermostat and said, "Do you want me to fix you a drink or get you a beer?"

"No thanks. Help yourself."

"Adam I need you to do something for me. Before you say no, hear me out."

"Okay. What is it?"

"Please stay here with me tonight. I desperately do not want to be alone after the most emotionally dreadful experience of my life. This was even worse than the day we buried my father. Caroline was my rock. Adam, I need you to be my rock today. Please be my rock today."

"I'll try, but we cannot sleep together."

"You're safe with me, Adam. At least for tonight. I promise."

"Maybe—but you're not safe with me, Diana."

"Risk it with me, Adam. We'll keep all our clothes on and stay here on the sofa. If anything gets physical, you go home to your condo. I cannot stay here alone tonight. Who else do I have to ask, besides you?"

"Esperanza?"

"No, I hardly know her. Nope."

"Don't you have a female friend from school or work?"

"There is a girl who often invites me to spend the weekend with her. But I'm not into her lifestyle."

"Oh. Oh, okay. But if anything happens between the two of us, it will only damage our relationship. Probably beyond repair."

"I know. Nothing will happen. Just sit with me. Hug me. Talk to me. Be with me. Cry with me. Pray with me. Just please don't leave me by myself. Do you want to watch a couple of video clips of Caroline?"

"What are you talking about?"

"I have two DVDs with home movies that have a few minutes of Caroline on them. On one, she's a bridesmaid at a wedding, and on another we were all on your sailboat at Lake Ray Hubbard last summer."

"No. I don't want to see those tonight. Let's play one of Caroline's favorite music CDs."

"Good idea. Caroline loved many of the old songs from the '50s, '60s, and '70s. You like The Moody Blues, so let's listen to their 'Seventh Sojourn' album. And then we'll watch one of her favorite movie DVDs. You've never watched 'Sneakers,' Me neither. Caroline tried to get me to watch it, but I never did. Let's watch it tonight. Okay?"

"Okay. That sounds like a good idea. As long as we can pause the music or the movie if we think of something to say about Caroline." Adam set up the CD player and DVD player so he could remotely control them from the couch. Even though he was a Moody Blues fan, Adam had never listened to the lyrics of their 'Seventh Sojourn' album. Diana heard most of the first song on the CD, then the music lulled her to sleep with her head on a pillow in Adam's lap. Adam listened intently to the lyrics.

The first song, "Lost in a Lost World," turned his thinking toward his God-Quest. Part of the lyrics were

Everywhere you go you see them searching,

    Everywhere you turn you feel the pain

Everyone is looking for the answer,

    Well look again, come on my friend

Love will find them in the end, Come on my friend

    We've got to bend, on our knees and say a prayer

Adam connected with the songs all the rest of the album, but he really became focused on the music in the middle of "When You're a Free Man." And he concentrated on all the lyrics to the last song: "I'm Just a Singer (In a Rock and Roll Band)."

Adam read from the CD insert, "The lyrics to this last song were written by John Lodge," but Diana had slept through the entire album. Adam looked at her face and thought, *You really do have a beautiful face, child—un, I mean, Kiddo,* and he kissed her on the forehead. Then his mind returned to things that matter for eternity.

Is it possible that God spoke to me through the lyrics of an old progressive rock-and-roll band? He suspected the correct answer was a loud "No!" But he thought *I'll have to remember to ask Juan about this.*

When the CD had finished, he started to play the movie—but he noticed that Diana was still sound asleep, so he just leaned back and reflected on his miraculous escape from certain death. *Diana and I will just have to watch "Sneakers" another time.*

Without waking her, he carried Diana into her bedroom and put her on her bed. Then he debated whether he should sleep in Caroline's bed or drive home at midnight. He chose to stay, but he closed and locked the bedroom door, took his shoes off, and slept fully dressed.

As Adam drifted off to sleep, he wondered, Am I asking the right people to help me come to know God? God please help me find reality—and you. Am I really searching for freedom? Freedom from what?

The next morning, he awakened before Diana and made a pot of coffee. Later that day, he called and asked Jackie how to get that album on his 16 GB iPod nano. She walked him through it over the phone. From then on, he listened to the album once or twice during the day and as he was falling asleep at night.

"Juan, can God speak to me through a secular song?'

"Probably. In his letter to Titus, Paul quoted a secular poet, Epimenides. But I would be careful. If you think God is speaking to you through nonbelievers, I'd make sure what they're saying is consistent with the Bible. Tell me what you've been experiencing."

"I first had this experience as Diana drove me from the hospital in Waco. A singer named Alison Krauss was singing a song entitled "There Is a Reason." I've listened to it over and over, and it is as if God is telling me to trust Jesus.

"A couple of nights ago, Diana and I listened to one of Caroline's old progressive rock CDs—The Moody Blues, you've probably not familiar with them."

"Did they sing, 'Nights in White Satin'?"

"Right, but not on this album. British group. Caroline liked old music from the 1940s, 1950s, 1960s, and 1970s. I don't recall listening to this album before, but Diana told me it was one of Caroline's favorites. She dozed off, but I was mesmerized. I might have zoned out a few times, too.

"The first song was 'Lost in a Lost World.' I didn't get every word of the song, but parts of it resonated with my God-Quest. The song painted a picture of selfish and prideful people fighting with each other. They sang,

Everywhere you go you see them searching,

Everywhere you turn you feel the pain

Everyone is looking for the answer,

Well look again, come on my friend

Love will find them in the end, Come on my friend

We've got to bend On our knees and say a prayer"

"I can see how you could interpret that in a spiritual way. Was that it? Or was there more?"

"Much more. Another part of the same song was

"Oh, can you see the world is pining

"Pining for someone who really cares enough to share his love

"With all of us, so we can be, An ever loving family

"That sure sounds like Jesus to me, Adam."

"That's what I thought too. As I listened to that album, I felt like God was speaking to me directly. Then I thought, *No. God speaks to us only through the Bible.* Isn't that what you taught me, Juan?"

"Not exactly. God speaks to people through his creation, other people, and through experiences—and a times, directly, either an audible voice or in your mind."

"Has God ever spoken to you in an audible voice, Juan?"

"Twice in my life. And the second time, I could see the words coming through the roof of my house and into my room."

"Wow. Like a vision?"

"I guess. We don't tell God how to communicate with us. So we need to be open to hearing from him in a variety of ways."

"Here." Adam handed Juan a piece of paper. "I printed out the lyrics from the last song for you to read. What do you think?"

"Give me a minute." Adam watched Juan's eyes and eyebrows for his reaction. Adam read:

I'm just a wandering on the face of this Earth

  Meeting so many people who are tryin' to be free

And while I'm traveling I hear so many words

  Language barriers broken, now we've found the key

And if you want the wind of change to blow about you

  And you're the only other person to know, don't tell me

I'm just a singer in a Rock 'n' Roll band

"The last verse was

"A thousand pictures can be drawn from one word

  "Only who is the artist? We got to agree

"A thousand miles can lead so many ways

  "Just to know who is driving, what a help it would be

"So if you want this world of yours to turn about you

  "And you can see exactly what to do

"Please tell me, I'm just a singer in a Rock 'n' Roll band

"Interesting. They're telling their fans not to expect that they have the answers to life's problems, the problems that plague humans. At least the song is a fair assessment of the human condition. And that is often a starting point for people who come to trust in the Savior. So what's your question?"

"Does the Bible tell us that God can speak through non-believers? Is there a precedent?"

"I already told you that St. Paul, in his letter to Titus, quoted the secular philosopher Epimenides. In the Old Testament book of Numbers, God used a donkey to speak to Balaam. I guess we should not limit God in any way that the Bible does not constrain him."

"This raises the question: Does the Bible limit God in any way, Juan?"

"Oh yes. The Bible tells us that God cannot lie and does not tempt people to do evil. Everything God does is always perfectly consistent with his character and purposes. Adam, you might try listening to music that helps you worship God rather than secular music. You may find that more beneficial to your faith journey."

"Yeah, I probably should. But it seems God is using what's available."

"Yeah. God does that too. I suggest you read parts of the Bible with Diana."

"Any part in particular, Juan?"

"Well not *The Song of Solomon*. Any one of the Gospels—do you have a favorite?"

"Not really."

Before long, Adam found radio stations on Sirius XM that played Christian music exclusively—and DFW had about thirty-odd local Christian radio stations, too. But he continued listening to country music almost half the time.

Chapter 5: Searching in Farmers Branch

Adam was hesitant as he drove to Farmer's Branch. When he saw a Christian bookstore, he wondered, *That's a Christian bookstore. I wonder why I've never noticed Christian bookstores before.* He parked and entered. He was hardly in the door when a clerk said, "Can I help you find something, sir?"

"Do you sell Bibles here? I'm looking for a Bible."

"Yes, sir. Please follow me." Adam was surprised to see a large bookcase full of an assortment of Bibles. "Are you looking for a particular translation? Is this for yourself, or a gift for someone else?"

He thought, *Hey, that's a great idea! If I find one I like, I'll buy one for Diana too.*

"I haven't decided yet. I want an English Bible. I'm not fluent enough in Spanish or any other language to read the Bible in a foreign language."

"I meant which English versions or translations are you looking for?'

"Sorry. I have no idea. But I want the best translation you have—not a cheap translation of the Bible. I want one that has all of God's truth in it."

Trying to hide a smile, the salesperson said, "Sir, the differences in prices of Bibles are generally due to the cost of the cover, binding, or ancillary materials like maps and a concordance."

"Well what translations are the best? Do you have one you recommend?"

"One popular translation is the King James Version, also known as the Authorized Version or just KJV. Another popular translation is the New International Version." He handed Adam a copy of each and waited for him to look over both of them.

"Okay. I definitely want one written in modern English. So what modern English versions do most people use?"

"Probably the New International Version is leading in popularity, but there are other good modern English translations and some paraphrases, too."

"What's the difference between a paraphrase and a translation?"

"Translations tend to more accurately say what the original language said. Some paraphrases tend toward denominational bias."

He said, "I don't want any denominational bias," although he was not positive what that meant. "Name some good translations for me."

"New American Standard Bible, New English Bible, New Revised Standard Bible, Contemporary English Bible, New English Translation, Holman Christian Standard Bible, and the Good News Translation."

"Wow. I never would have guessed there were that many English Bibles!"

"Sir, that's not even half of them. Tell me about yourself and what you want to do with the Bible, and I might be able to guide you to a suitable choice."

"Okay. I've been an atheist for years, but a recent experience provokes me to investigate the claims of Christianity. I don't recall reading the Bible until recently, but often I cannot figure out what God's trying to tell me."

"Are you learning Greek or Hebrew?"

"No."

"In that case, I would not recommend the NASB."

"Why not?"

"I find the English unnatural and wooden—and difficult to understand at times. But it's helpful to a person studying Hebrew or Greek. You might get a parallel Bible."

"What's that?"

"Two or more translations, side-by-side, for comparison."

"So you just choose the one you like?"

"Well, the meaning is usually the same, even if the words are different.

"Or, you might like one of the study Bibles. *The NIV Study Bible* and *The NET Bible* are both good. But you must remember that the notes at the bottom of each page are not part of the inspired, authoritative Bible— they're modern comments on the text."

"Yes. That's good. Let me get one of each of those two, please."

"Do you want a red-letter edition?" Adam's face signaled a lack of comprehension, so the salesman continued, "The words of Jesus are printed in red."

"Jesus spoke English?"

With a smile, the salesman said, "The words of Jesus are translated into English and printed in red." The salesman opened a red-letter edition to John to show him.

Adam hesitated for a moment, and then said, "No thanks."

"Very good, sir. Binding?" Again Adam's silence and face revealed he did not understand the one word question, so, with a small sigh, the salesman explained, "Paperback, hardback, or leather cover?"

"Leather."

"What color? Black, burgundy, blue, or white?"

"One blue and one burgundy—doesn't matter which is which color. I just want to be able to distinguish them from a distance."

"Thank you, sir. Would you like the cover embossed?"

"Embossed?"

"With a name, sir. In gold letters. Only $5.00 extra for each book— unless the name is over twelve letters long."

He spoke kindly, "No, thank you." But he thought, *If that boy asks me one more question, I'm walking out and ordering from Amazon!*

As they walked toward the cash register, he saw a table with an assortment of bumper stickers with Christian slogans. He stopped and read one or two. The young salesman said, "This one is my favorite:

'God said it. I believe it. That settles it.' What do you think, sir? Would you like to buy this to put on your car?"

Adam asked the salesman, "Are you a Christian?"

"Oh, yes sir. I've been a Christian all of my life."

"Well I'm not a Christian, but if I were, I might ask you, 'if God said it, wouldn't that settle it even if you did not believe it'?"

"Oh. I guess you're right."

Then Adam saw one that said, "God is my co-pilot."

The salesman saw him reading that one and incorrectly guessed that he liked it. Remembering Adam's response to the previous bumper sticker, the salesman hesitated, then said, "Do you want to buy that one, sir."

"No thanks, but maybe you can help me understand it."

"Yes sir. I'll try."

"Isn't the co-pilot the second in command? My Christian friend, Juan, told me that Jesus is the King of kings and rules a Christian's life—and I think Juan knows what he's saying. I'm not a Christian, so I don't fully understand Christianity—but I sure don't understand why this store sells these bumper stickers. Could you explain it to me?"

"Only that this is a business, so I guess we sell anything Christians are likely to buy." Adam suppressed his urge to ask him to point him toward the bottled liquor. Instead, he paid for his purchase, walked back to his car, and continued looking for the church he planned to visit.

With the aid of his GPS, he found the church, parked, and walked into the brick building. He followed the signs to the church office,

"Excuse me, ma'am. I'm looking for the minister. Is he in?"

"I'm Rev. Sofia Bishop. It's nice to meet you. How can I help you?"

"My apologies. Rev. Bishop, I'm Adam Bowers."

She said, "No apology is needed, Mr. Bowers. Please just call me Sister Bishop."

"Yes ma'am. Sis. Bishop, I've been an atheist or an agnostic for years. But I recently had an experience that has motivated me to me investigate the evidence for God's existence. I'm starting with Christian groups. If I don't find the answers I'm looking for in Christianity, I may investigate other religions—if I don't lose interest first."

She said, "I assume it's obvious that I believe the God of the Bible exists and has been revealed in the creation, in Christ Jesus, and in the Bible." Adam nodded his head to confirm her assumption.

"I plan to visit your church this Sunday morning. Is that a good idea?"

"Yes, we welcome you. We're an extremely diverse group—people of different races, different nationalities, and different socioeconomic levels. We are Pentecostal in belief and in practice. The gifts of the Holy Spirit are often active in our services—but not always. I usually preach and minister in the power of the Spirit. Sometimes God ministers in other ways, and I don't get to preach."

Adam did not comprehend the significance of what Bishop said, so he replied politely, "I've never heard a woman preach. I look forward to being here."

The next Sunday morning, Adam and Diana went to hear Sis. Bishop. They liked many aspects of the service, but he also jotted down questions to ask Juan when they met on Tuesday. As they were leaving, Adam and Diana greeted Sis. Bishop.

"Welcome, friends. Was this your first experience in a Pentecostal church?"

"Yes, for both of us. Sis. Bishop, this is Diana Norris, a very close friend."

They exchanged the obligatory "It's so nice to meet you" greetings.

"May I ask you both a question?"

Diana said, "Sure, as long as you won't be too upset if we decline to answer."

"The answer may be too personal, so I promise I won't be too upset if you decline. Why did neither of you share your dream with the church and hear God interpret if for you?" Adam and Caroline looked at each other, wondering how Sis. Bishop knew about their dreams—wondering if the other person had told her about their dreams.

This awkward question did not facilitate conversation, but Adam finally explained, "Number one, we're first-time visitors and do not know anyone here, and, number two, our dreams are very personal." Diana quickly nodded to agree with this reply.

"And number three—and here I speak only for myself—I had no confidence that the interpretation of my recurring dream would come from God—no offense intended."

"And none taken. I appreciate candor, Mr. Bowers."

Diana asked, "How did you know that we've had recurring dreams that have bothered us?"

"Well, my dear, either your faces betrayed you, or God gave me discernment—or a bit of both. Adam, may I pray and ask God to heal your mind so your memory is restored?"

"That would be great! I wish he would. If you think it would help, please pray." His voice had the sound of hopeful excitement.

Sis. Bishop put a small amount of olive oil from the Holy Land on Adam's forehead and began praying. She prayed loudly in English and in tongues for Adam. She put both hands over his ears and shook his head so violently that Adam had to sit down in a pew. He thought, *Wow. She's strong. One more twist and I would have been flat on the floor.*

"Are you healed, Adam? Can you tell any difference in your memory?"

"Just a moment, ma'am, I'm dizzy. Diana, can you test my memory?"

Diana said, "Do you recall the name of your favorite high school teacher?"

"No. Not yet."

"What's your Social Security Number?"

"Sorry. I cannot remember."

"What was your father's middle name?"

"Three strikes and I'm out. I don't remember. So I guess my memory has not returned. Sorry."

Sis. Bishop encouraged him, "The Bible says people must have faith in order for God to answer our prayers. You should publicly confess that God has healed your memory, Adam."

"What do you mean by 'publicly confess that God has healed'?"

"Glorify God by telling all your friends that we prayed for God to restore your memory and you believe that God has healed you."

"But I cannot recall things that I should know. People will soon know what I say is false. How will this glorify God?"

"You are speaking in faith of things that we do not see yet, but we believe—by faith in God—that will very soon be true."

"Couldn't I just tell friends that I'm hoping God will heal me?"

"No. that's not the same as genuine believing faith."

"God will change your mind soon, Adam. I'm patient and have faith in God that he will change your heart and mind."

"Before we leave, Adam said, "Sis. Bishop, how do I come to know God as you know God?"

She answered, "God has a greater desire for you to know him than you have to know him, Adam. Why are you so reluctant to allow God to find you?"

"I guess for at least two reasons; first I have amnesia and do not know who I am, or who I was." Rev. Bishop's face revealed her empathy at Adam's condition.

"And second, God miraculously rescued me from certain death in a plane crash. I fear God made a mistake—I think he rescued the wrong person, and when he discovers that, he'll come for me." Then he made a buzzing sound like a bug zapper electrocuting a large horse fly.

"Relax. God did not make a mistake. What makes you think he made a mistake?"

"Because I've discovered that I've been an outspoken atheist all of my adult life."

"Adam, God loves atheists as much as he loves any other person. Christ died for you as much as he died for me, Diana, Oral Roberts, or for Billy Graham."

"Let me tell you what I tell people who come to church here, but are struggling with their faith.

"First, pray without ceasing—pray through. Pray until God gives you the answer you need.

"Second, praise God, because he inhabits the praises of his people.

Third, seek until you receive the second blessing—the Baptism in the Holy Spirit—and then exercise the gifts of the Holy Spirit.

Smiling, she said, "I'm sure that, if you'll continue coming to church here, you'll personally come to know God—soon and very soon."

Now that's a self-serving-answer, he thought to himself.

That Tuesday evening at dinner, Adam told Juan and Esperanza about their experience. "Juan, last Sunday we went to an independent Pentecostal church. Do you know Pastor Sophia Bishop?"

"No. I know of her, but I've never met her. And I've never been to that church."

"Juan, you told me that you're Pentecostal and Catholic. Should I become Pentecostal and Catholic too? I'm curious, what does 'Pentecostal/Charismatic Catholic' mean? Is it a secret religious society or fraternity?"

Juan smiled as he said, "No. The short answer is this: Pentecostals are Christians who believe that God still imparts to believers the gifts of the Holy Spirit recorded in the New Testament. Some other Christians teach that the gifts of the Holy Spirit ended with the death of the Apostles or with the completion of the Canon of Scripture, the Bible. There are two reasons that I'm not a cessationist. First, I cannot find the Bible teaches it, and second, I've experienced some of the gifts of the Holy Spirit.

"Should you become Pentecostal too? Well, first become a Christian. Then, my advice to you is that you seek the Holy Spirit of God, the Giver of Gifts, and allow him to gift you when, where, and how he pleases. And don't treat cessationists as if they're less spiritual, second class Christians.

"Should you become Catholic? I have no idea. You're asking the wrong person. Find out what God wants you to be. I'm probably Catholic only because I grew up in the Catholic Church.

"Some of my cessationist Christian friends think Pentecostals deny the Trinity of God. Most do not; one group does. Others think Pentecostals teach a person must speak in tongues in order to be saved. That is also not true."

"Tell me, Adam, what did you think of Rev. Bishop and that church?"

"I liked the diversity. There seemed to be no distinction between Latinos, Anglos, and African Americans. I also liked their energy. They worshipped wholeheartedly, unashamedly, with raised hands, dancing with 'reckless abandon'—at first it was a little off-putting, but they seemed to be sincere. I call it 'aerobic worship.' I did not know any of the songs they sang—oh, except the first verse of "Amazing Grace.""

"Did you have any negative observations?"

"Maybe a few. At times they seemed to worship the Bible instead of God."

"I doubt they really worship the Bible—a deep reverence for Scripture is not unusual among people who embrace the Bible as divinely inspired. Anything else?"

"When they prayed for healing, they put oil on that person's forehead and everyone touched that person as they prayed. Oh, and one man said his aunt was in the hospital; she had sent a handkerchief and asked everyone to put oil on it and pray for her healing. He was to take the handkerchief back to her hospital bed. I admit that I don't understand this. How do you explain it? I thought it was a superstition."

"This is not a habit of mine, but it is based on what Luke wrote in Acts 19:12. Luke tells us that sick people were healed when they touched Paul's apron or handkerchief. Don't worry about that now. What else happened at church?"

"At one point, a large lady stood and spoke in tongues. When she finished, a moment later, another lady stood shouted out, 'Thus saith the Lord....' I was spooked and had goose bumps all over my body, and I thought I sensed the presence of God's Spirit."

"Goose bumps are due to the contraction of the arrector pilli muscles in your skin—they're not a 'Holy Ghost Detector.' Is that all she said? 'Thus saith the Lord....'"

"No, but I cannot quote all of what she said. What followed sounded like God was mad as Hay-Yil with the people who go to that church and was about to severely punish them for being neither hot nor cold. I thought, *God, I'm just a first-time visitor here—not a member!* "I sure hope he can read my thoughts. I don't want God to think I'm tepid—or a member of that church."

"He does know your thoughts, Adam. Again Pentecostals see this as a message in tongues—usually thought to be a 'heavenly language'—followed by an interpretation. In his letters, Paul warns leaders to evaluate the message and interpretation, but I've never heard any leader do that. One leader told me that this would make Christians reluctant to manifest the gifts. I thought this might be a good reason to obey Scripture."

"At one point, Rev. Bishop asked if anyone had a dream to share. They have something called a 'Ministry of Interpreting Dreams.' One person told of a dream she'd had recently. Neither the dream nor the interpretation made much sense to me—both seemed trivial."

"Maybe it was meaningful only to the person who had the dream."

"Ah, that is a possibility. Then the chairman of the deacons went to the front of the sanctuary and asked the deacons to collect donations to the church. But first he took several minutes to rebuke church members for not giving enough money to pay the mortgage, the electric bill, and the pastor. I suspect this was why God was mad at them.

"Then, at the end of the worship service, Sis. Bishop asked people needing prayer to come to the front, and she'd pray for them. When she put her hand on their foreheads, they fell to the floor moaning softly. One man did not fall. It seemed to me that he just refused to fall. Rude, huh?" Juan did not respond to his question, and Adam continued.

"Sis. Bishop seemed to stress the 'baptism of the Holy Spirit' and 'the gifts of the Spirit' more than a personal salvation experience. Oh, that reminds me: what does *sanctification* mean? Sis. Bishop emphasized the need for personal sanctification. She stressed that suffering sanctifies us. Suffering doesn't sound like something I'd sign up for today. There's got to be a better way."

"Sanctification is a maturation process of a believer becoming more like Jesus. According to the Bible, God's Spirit uses all of life's circumstances—good or bad—to produce the character of Christ in us. God's way is always the best way, and may be the only way too. "So…do you plan to visit them again next Sunday?"

"No. Diana usually goes with me, and that church made her uncomfortable. I promised a friend I'd visit a huge church in Carrollton—

she called it a Megachurch. They must be doing something right if they're huge. Right?"

"I sure hope so.

"Adam, how often are you reading the Bible?"

"Generally, every week I read one of the Gospels, the Book of Acts, and all of the letters. Then the next week I read a different Gospel, the Book of Acts, and all of the letters. This week, I'm reading Luke, the Book of Acts, and all of the letters. I tried to read Revelation, but didn't understand it at all. It is not like the rest of the New Testament; it's weird."

"True, it is different. We'll talk about that book sometime. What translation are you reading?"

Have you ever heard of *Good News for Modern Man*?"

"Sure, also known as Today's English Version or The Good News Bible, I think."

"I like reading it most, but sometimes I read the Contemporary English Version and The New International Version.

"Great. Good choices."

"Juan, am I wrong to think everyone should have an experience similar to mine in order to be a real Christian?"

"How similar? Maybe God works in the lives of different people differently. Nowhere in the New Testament do we hear St. Paul insist that a person must have his Damascus Road experience in order to become a Christian. St. Thomas did not insist everyone must have his experience either. We must be careful not to usurp the work of God's Spirit. He draws people to himself. He convicts people of sin. He convinces people that he died and rose again. And he alone forgives sin and convinces people that they are forgiven. Our task is to proclaim his Gospel of forgiveness and sanctification, God has to do the rest."

"So, Juan, you're Pentecostal. What insights do you have for me from our visit with Sis. Bishop?"

"First, the positive. I think all Christians should be led by God's Holy Spirit in accord with the teaching of Scripture—whether we've had a Pentecostal experience or not.

"I do believe that the gifts of the Holy Spirit are important to the local church and to individual believers—and that the New Testament teaches us that they are intended to glorify God, not the human who exercises the gift.

"I do think ordinary Christians can understand most of the Bible without a scholarly interpretation. This is especially true when it comes to grasping God's offer of forgiveness. So, much of the time, all we need are 'surface or simple' interpretations. For some Bible passages and doctrines, perhaps a correct understanding is a little more difficult to comprehend.

"I bought a book for you that you might find helpful." Adam accepted the book and read the title, *Grasping God's Word* by Duvall and Hayes."

A couple of weeks later, Juan gave Adam a copy of *Reading the Bible for All Its Worth* by Fee & Stuart. He'd highlighted a line on page 61-62: "The Basic Rule: A text cannot mean what it never could have meant to its author or his readers."

Juan said, "In my mind, these two books are connected. Duvall and Hayes book is predicated on this statement of "The Basic Rule" by Fee and Stuart. Let me explain what they're getting at here, Adam. Many people think some parts of Scripture were intended only for those people in that time and place. I call it 'them/then/there'—in a minute I'll give you an example. So, at times, our task is to determine if God intended a passage to transcend culture and time and he intended for it to be universally applied—not only for 'them/then/there,' but also for 'us/now/here.' And Bible-believing Christians don't always agree on whether a proposition is 'culturally bound' or not.

"So, in his letter to Timothy, Paul tells him that women are not to be teachers in the church. Some Christians read this as applying to all Christians, regardless of time, place, or culture. Other Christians think Paul—and God—were giving this instruction to the Church in Ephesus. The underlying reason for this interpretation is a little too long and complex to tell you now, but this issue has caused more than one argument over church government or doctrine. Generally, each camp in this argument thinks they alone know God's Truth."

Juan said, "If you like *Grasping God's Word*, I'll get you the sequel: *Living God's Word* by the same authors.

"Here's my opinions on a couple of negatives. I've never been awed by what I call *trivial miracles*—like a sick cat being healed or a dead hamster being raised from the dead.' We don't find Jesus performing such trivial miracles in the New Testament. Certainly it's not impossible, but I don't find such things recorded in the Bible.

"I wish Pentecostals emphasized the fruit of the Spirit in Galatians 5 as much as we emphasize the gifts of the Spirit in 1 Corinthians 12. Most of the Bible is easily understood, but sometimes we find a passage that seems to defy our understanding."

Adam said, "Can you give me an example?"

"I'll give you a few and tell you why it's a problem. In 1 Corinthians 8, Paul talks about food offered to idols. This is a minor problem for some Christians because we have no contemporary parallel in our culture. So we try to extract a principle and then apply this principle to our own culture. Paul challenged Christians in Corinth that even though they are free to eat food that had been offered to an idol, they should not do that in a way that weakens the faith of a less mature Christian. The guiding principle is one of love and can be applied to every human culture—including ours."

"So, I know I can be a genuine Christian and drink beer or wine, but if I do that in a way that weakens the faith of another believer, it would be wrong?"

"Right. Love is what we do to others, not just what we say or what we feel.

"Another problem is what Paul writes in 1 Corinthians 15:29. The NIV translates it

> Now if there is no resurrection, what will those do who are
> baptized for the dead? If the dead are not raised at all, why are
> people baptized for them?

"Again, Adam, baptism saving anyone—living or dead—seems like salvation-by-works—which the New Testament clearly repudiates. And further: Can one person do anything to change the eternal destiny of another person? We don't find this taught elsewhere in Scripture. And that's what makes it a problem-passage."

Adam said, "So, what do we do with this passage? Why didn't Paul explain what he meant in the letter?"

"He didn't need to. The recipients already knew the practice and what it meant—and what it did not mean."

"Do we have any reasonable explanation for this passage."

"Maybe. Some scholars think it referred to a person coming to faith and dying—maybe as a martyr—before he or she could be baptized. This is what happened to my sister. She confessed Christ as Lord and Savior about twenty-four hours before she died in a hospital. Under the right circumstances, I would not hesitate to be baptized as her proxy. It would just be a testimony of her confession of Christ Jesus as Lord and Savior—but it would not change her standing before God."

"Paul's letters also provide other examples of problem passages. In 1 Timothy 2:15, he writes that "women will be saved through childbearing.""

"Did Paul mean that childbearing saves a woman? That seems to contradict the clear teaching of the Bible that salvation does not depend on good works—it cannot be earned. It is offered to people without merit."

"Did Paul mean that Christian women would not die in giving birth? Certainly godly Christian women have died in childbirth."

"So how is this problem solved?"

"I'm not sure that it is completely solved to everyone's satisfaction. But I'll tell you how some attempt to solve it. You might call it smoke and mirrors.

"Dr. Fee and other scholars argue that this sentence connects back to a reference to Eve. As Eve sinned and earned God's punishment, so God's salvation will come through womankind, in the form of the Messiah."

"Do you think that's what the Christians in Ephesus thought it meant?"

"No idea. But at least you understand why the Bible has some problem passages, and how Bible scholars might help ordinary Christians understand the Bible better."

"I did not realize interpreting the Bible has so many pitfalls to avoid."

"True, but recall my first statement: Most of the God's message in the Bible is easily understood by ordinary Christians. I'll just give you one more from the New Testament—but it's equally applicable to the Old Testament.

"Another problem involves knowing what the original human author intended by a given word. Some Greek words are found only once in the New Testament manuscripts. We call them *hapax legomena*, —or more simply, *hapax*. The term can be applied to a word in any body of literature, so we have Pauline hapaxes, Shakespearian hapaxes, New Testament hapaxes, Bible hapaxes, and Encyclopedia Britannica hapaxes.

"By definition, a hapax is found only once in a body of literature, they do not exist in multiple contexts, so translators cannot compare other usages in the Bible and infer which meaning an author intended from the range of meaning of that word. In that case, they look for that word in secular texts written about that same time.

"Here's an example of a hapax. Paul refers to himself in 1 Corinthians 15:8 as an *ektroma*. In this passage, Paul is assuring Christians that Jesus was literally resurrected—and thus, we can be confident that God will also raise us from the grave. He writes that the risen Jesus was seen by many people, and he writes,

> Then he appeared to James, then to all the apostles. Last of all, as to one untimely born, he appeared also to me.

"The translators of the NIV translated the word *ektroma* was as 'untimely born.' But some translators prefer to translate it as 'abortion.' No one questions that he's using *ektroma* metaphorically. But it's the only place we find this Greek word in Paul's letters. Alas, we don't have another case in the Pauline epistles to compare it with and decide if Paul was using it it another way.

"Notice that his passage is not connected to any crucial doctrine of Christianity—so I won't call it a problem passage. We're just not positive what Paul intended by the word."

"What you're teaching me makes me nervous."

"Why's that?"

"I fear I'll misinterpret the Bible, and God will punish me for it."

Juan smiled, "Well, relax. You almost certainly will misunderstand parts of the Bible. But the Gospel of salvation through faith in the atoning death of Jesus of Nazareth is very plainly revealed in the Bible. And God's love, favor, and forgiveness do not depend on your having a perfectly accurate understanding of every passage of Scripture. If it did, none of us would stand a chance."

"Help me to understand what sin is, Juan. Exactly what is sin?"

"The Bible does not try to prove people are sinners, it simply points it out repeatedly. For example, in this letter to the church in Rome, St Paul wrote:

"for all have sinned and fall short of the glory of God (Romans 3:23)

"And in John's letter,

"If we claim we have not sinned, we make him out to be a liar and his word is not in us. 1 John 1:10

"If I told you that I forgive your sins, it wouldn't mean anything. I have no authority to forgive any sin. But Jesus Christ claimed to have that authority in Matthew 9:6.

"I want you to know that the Son of Man has authority on earth to forgive sins.

"The Old Testament condemned rebellion against God, for example in Deuteronomy 9:7 and Joshua 1:18. And the New Testament gives what amounts to definitions:

Everyone who sins breaks the law; in fact, sin is lawlessness. 1 John 3:4

All wrongdoing is sin. 1 John 5:17

If anyone, then, knows the good they ought to do and doesn't do it, it is sin for them. James 4:17

"So a person can sin by doing nothing?"
"True. Doing nothing when you should be doing something is sin."

"Juan, I've heard you use the phrase *surface reading* in reference to interpreting the Bible. What do you mean by *surface reading*?"
"Maybe this is best illustrated. Years ago, a Christian group argued that we should not have Christmas trees. To support their position, they quoted Jeremiah 10:3-4

For the customs of the peoples are delusion;
Because it is wood cut from the forest,
The work of the hands of a craftsman with a cutting tool.
They decorate it with silver and with gold;
They fasten it with nails and with hammers
So that it will not totter. (NASB)

They applied this to the Christmas tree and concluded Christmas trees were a form of idolatry. But does anyone worship a Christmas tree? Probably not. Instead of extracting from the passage what the original human author and the divine author were trying to say, these people read into the passage their own cultural meaning.

"Is that common?"

"Probably more common than we like to admit. Another example has to do with tattoos. In Leviticus 19:28, the New American Standard Bible says,

> You shall not make any cuts in your body for the dead nor make
> any tattoo marks on yourselves: I am the Lord.

A surface reading usually ignores the context and the meaning the original audience probably understood, and interprets only the English translation as understood by modern readers. In this passage, the phrase 'for the dead' refers to people trying to communicate with the dead or ancestral worship. It had nothing to do with modern surgery or the current fad among young people to adorn themselves with body piercings or body art."

Chapter 6: Minding His Own Business

Adam felt like he was in a bizarre surreal dream when he entered Terry Realty around 6:00 P.M. Voices sounded like they were echoing in a large pipe. In his mind, he recognized that this is where he worked for a few years—the people around him were colleagues and friends—but in his heart, he felt like they were all foreigners. His brain thought *these are* my *friends;* his gut insisted *be very cautious—these are aliens and I'm in a strange place.*

The conference room did not look familiar to him, but he knew it was. It would comfortably seat a dozen people—the large conference room would seat twice that many. Fortunately, everyone wore name tags with both first and last names—as he did. Adam tried to talk with one person at a time, but at times he had three people around him, pressing him with questions and accolades.

Since Adam did not preside over the meeting, one of the older gentlemen took control of the group and functioned as an emcee. "Adam, would you like for us to give you a short biographical sketch of who we are and what we do?"

"Yes, thank you. I think that would be helpful. And after that, who will tell me who I am and what I do?" Everyone laughed at this—just a bit nervously.

A lady in her early forties spoke up, "Thanks, Skip. I'm Tina Bartlett, and I'm the office manager, Mr. Bowers. I do almost everything except clean the toilets and sell properties. I also manage our onsite managers for our rental properties." Adam suspected that she was annoyed with the way Skip took charge; maybe thought he had usurped her position—even if he had longevity.

Tina looked to her left and a younger lady said, "Mr. Bowers, I'm Jackie Hall, the receptionist and assistant to Tina. I generally do anything Tina asks me to do. I also assist sales people every way I can and see to the comforts of our clients."

The self-appointed emcee said, "I am Michael Masters, but friends call me 'Skip.' You and I have been friends for years, Adam. We were not room mates at UT, but we were close friends, and we've been working together here since 'Day One.' I'm the Vice-President of Sales and own eleven percent of the company stock. I sell, coordinate with Tina, and manage our seven junior sales persons. I also work with you on our corporate advertising."

The seven other sales people—two ladies and five men—introduced themselves with a couple of well-chosen sentences. Adam could not help but notice that the two ladies were physically attractive and dressed very stylishly—or so he thought.

Jackie saw a questioning look on Adam's face, so she continued the conversation by asking him, "Are you wondering what you do here, Mr. Bowers?"

"Yes. I guess I'm in sales too—right?"

"You're right, you do sell, but you're also our boss. You're the owner of one of the top, most financially successful realty in the northern sector of the Metroplex."

"Which one is that?'

"This one, boss, this one!" Adam was embarrassed that he'd missed her point.

"That means I've got a lot to learn. You folks better hope that I regain my memory soon! Where'd we get the name 'Terry'?"

Skip said, "It was your mother's maiden name before she got married."

Tina corrected him, "She didn't have a maiden name until after she married."

Skip ignored her correction. While the group was chuckling about that, one of the younger, more witty salesmen said, "Mr, Bowers, I hope you remember that you promised me a pay raise last week, boss." The laughter and the repeated phrase of "Me too, boss," convinced Adam that he was being teased, and he laughed with them.

After the laughter subsided, Tina completed the overview of Terry Realty with this statement, "TR also owns some rental houses and a few apartment complexes too. And Jackie and I train onsite managers, keep the original of all leases, give photocopies to the onsite managers, and collect the rent from the managers. If repairs cost over a thousand dollars, we consult with Skip, you, or both."

All of them spoke at once, so that Adam didn't understand any one of them, but he could tell they meant to encourage him. They wanted to ask him about the accident, but they wisely refrained. Adam did not exercise the same wisdom when he asked the group, "Did any of you know my wife?"

Skip hesitated and then said, "I did. I was best man at y'all's wedding in Alabama." A few days later, Skip showed him a photo of the wedding party, but it did not provoke any memories.

Tina stood and announced, "Now, if you will all follow me into the large conference room, a catered meal awaits us. BBQ beef and pork, baked beans, tater salad, coleslaw, Cokes on ice and cold beer—and banana pudding for dessert." None of them had to be told twice.

They pushed Adam to the front of the line. He was surprised that Diana appeared on the scene. "Where'd you come from, Kiddo?"

"I couldn't pass up free food from Lockhart's Smokehouse—and you."

Adam had seen some legal papers in his desk at his condo, and one of them was a divorce decree dated years ago. From this he learned he had wed Sherry Carter, she owned five percent of the TR stock, and they had no children. Later he asked Diana if she knew what had become of Sherry. "I heard she'd remarried and moved out of town." Diana helped him search the Internet, but they found no trace of her.

After they had finished their meal, Tina was showing Adam and Diana around the building, which was a remodeled house that was built a couple of years after World War 1. Tina and Jackie were animated as they described the history of TR and how it had grown from two people to become a major Realtor in that part of north Dallas.

Then Adam asked Tina and Jackie, "Do either of you know what became of Sherry, my first wife?" The question puzzled both of them.

Jackie did not answer, but looked at Tina as if to say, "You answer this."

Finally Tina said, "Sherry remarried and moved away. I haven't seen her in years. Why did you ask?

"I'm really not sure. I guess there's no way I could contact her, with her having remarried. It might prove awkward."

Tina and Jackie agreed with him, "You're probably right."

The next day Diana had an email from Jackie that simply read, "Sherry Meadows," followed by an address in Houston and a telephone number.

Diana waited another day before she asked Adam, "What would you want to do if you could locate Sherry?"

He said, "I cannot recall anything about her or our marriage. I calculated from the dates on the court papers that we were together almost four years and had no children. Maybe she is a key to my regaining my lost memory. I'd like to call her—but what if her new husband answered the phone? If we find her, would you help me call her?"

Diana asked him, "Why do you want to call her?"

He answered, "I've been asking myself that question—repeatedly. I've also asked myself, 'What do you want to ask her?' Part of the answer is that I'm hoping a conversation with her would help me recover my memory. But is that the only reason I want to call her? There's probably more to my wish, but I don't know what it is. People rarely do something for a single reason. I'd wish her all the joy and love in the world."

"Jackie found her address and phone number, and she emailed them to me. I'll agree to help you—on the condition that I'm present, and we use a speaker phone. If the call goes south, you say good-bye, and we hang up." He eagerly agreed to her conditions, and Diana called that number.

Diana said, "I'll call. If Sherry says she does not want to talk to you— what then?"

"Just let her know about the accident and my memory problems, and I wish her well. Oh, and say that I hope she has forgiven me for anything wrong I've ever done to her. I will say nothing unless she agrees to talk to me. And you can promise her that I do not have her address or phone number, so I won't try to contact her ever again."

Adam became very tense as they heard the phone in Houston ring. Then a voice—a lady's voice—said, "Hello." Adam did not recognize her voice.

"Yes ma'am. This is an operator in Dallas," she lied, "would you accept a call to Sherry from an Adam Bowers?"

After a short pause, the feminine voice said, "This is a collect long distance call?"

"No. Mr. Bowers is paying for the call. But he's not sure Sherry is willing to talk to him."

"This is Sherry Meadows. Yes, I'll take that call." And Diana handed the phone to Adam.

"Sherry, this is Adam. I was in an accident, and I have amnesia."

"I know—I saw the news on TV about the accident and saw your picture as the only survivor. Are you doing well?"

"Very well, thank you, except for the lack of a memory. Sherry, I don't remember anything about you or our marriage. I hope I didn't mistreat or abuse you in any way."

"You didn't, well, no more than I mistreated you. We grew apart. We had different interests and different values. I was expecting a baby, and you thought marriage was the only chivalrous solution. Our baby was born and died the same day. He was premature. Neither of us ever recovered from that tragedy. I blamed God, and you blamed both me and God.

"We grew apart and finally gave up and divorced, and I moved back to the Houston area. Gary and I have been married for years, and we have two boys and two girls—elementary school, middle school, and high school."

"Day-Yim That's great! I'm happy for you both. Is there anything that you might tell me with any chance of restarting my memory? Anything at all?"

"Not really. Oh, here's one. Do you know where you got the habit of saying 'Day-Yim' as two words?"

"No. Is there a story there?"

"Just a short story. You told me that when you were a youngster in southern Alabama, your maternal grandparents raised you. You and your mom lived with her parents in southern Alabama while your father worked offshore on an oil rig in the Gulf of Mexico. You often heard your maternal grandfather use three expletives. He pronounced them as two syllables—really, as two words: 'Day-Yim,' 'She-Yit,' and 'Hay-Yil'. And you imitated him. This became an affectation and endeared you to your high school buddies." Diana and Adam found this mildly amusing.

Diana asked, "Didn't he have a better quirk for you to imitate?"

"No. Nothing I remember.

"Thanks for telling me that, Sherry. Please apologize to your husband for my calling you. I promise that I won't call you again. Oh, before you hang up—do y'all go to church anywhere?"

"What! Who are you, and what have you done with Adam Bowers? Yes we do, Adam. As a matter of fact, we're both very active in our church, and Gary works with The Gideons. Why'd you ask that?"

Adam did not answer her question. He said, "Great! That's wonderful! Uh, what's a Gideon?"

"It's a group who distributes Bibles to people. They put Bibles in hotel and motel rooms and in the waiting rooms of doctors and dentists. Do you want me to have him send you a Bible?"

"What kind of Bible is it? How much does it cost?"

"It's a Holy Bible. Cost? Nothing."

"Okay. I guess I can afford that. I'll ask Diana to give you my address."

"I can just send it to Terry Realtors—if the address has not changed."

'It's the same, but don't send it there. I'll let Diana give you my home address."

"Okay. Is Diana your wife?"

"No. We're just friends. Her sister, my fiancée, was killed in the plane crash." Diana was miffed by his 'just friends' response and tried not to let it show.

"Oh, Adam, I'm so sorry."

"Thanks. Here's Diana." He handed the phone to her and lost himself in thought over Sherry.

He thought, *Sherry sounded so pleased that I called her. Her life seems to be so fulfilled. I wish I could meet her and Gary and their children. I'm so relieved that she's doing well. I hope she's found some measure of happiness.*

When Diana finished giving Adam's mailing address at work to Sherry, she hung up the phone and said, "Well. Did anything she said jump-start your memory, Adam? Did you recognize her voice?"

"Not yet. She had a different accent, almost foreign—is she from another country? Is she a northerner? How did she sound to you, Diana?"

"She sounded mature, cheerful, sincere, and content. She sounded sincerely pleased to hear your voice. And the accent is leftover from her childhood in New Hampshire. I think she was a young adult when her job moved her to Houston. Why what did you think?"

"The same. How could she be happy to hear from me? She must know something I don't know. Do you think that she thought that her life is much better than mine? Was she glad that we aren't still married?"

"I heard nothing that sounded like that, Adam."

Adam thought a moment, and then said, "I wish her happiness."

A few days later, Adam received a Bible from Gary and Sherry in the mail. Since it was the New Living Translation—a different translation than the one he bought—the gift motivated him to get busy reading it. He didn't tell Diana or Juan, but he would read one of the Gospels, Acts, and all of the letters each week. He tried to read Revelation, but recognized that he did not understand it, so he decided to save it until he understood the Gospels and the Epistles better.

Chapter 7: Searching in Carrollton

Adam had not gone to church at all last Sunday. He told Diana that he didn't feel well, but he was just being lazy.

Tina told Adam about a large church in Carrollton. She did attend that church, but she did visit there once. Tina really liked the orchestra and choir performances. Instead of meeting and interviewing the pastor, Adam read about this church on their web site. The more Adam learned about this church, the more he liked the idea of visiting it. He thought, *they won't embarrass all the visitors by making us pin a crimson ribbon on our chests.* He really liked the fact that over 5,000 people attended this church. *The fact that this church is big indicates that God is blessing it. They must be teaching and preaching the truth. I'll bet this is where Jesus would go to church if he was visiting Texas.*

For the first time since the plane crash, Adam drove a vehicle. He met Diana at her apartment and asked, "Do you want to drive?"

"I will if you want me to."

"We'll see. I feel confident. Shout if I drive poorly."

"Okay. By the way, I like that shirt with those slacks."

"I went by Penny's and bought a few shirts that had some color. Do you think it's too flashy?"

"No. I think it looks great on you."

Pastor Armstrong was bombastic and emphasized the fact that this church is a Protestant church. He was loud and included the word *excited* in almost every sentence, and the congregation applauded every few minutes. They applauded the children's choir, the adult choir, the announcement that 'ushers will now receive the offering,' and the beautiful and shapely young lady in skin-tight pants who read a passage from the Bible. They always said they were clapping for God, but Adam was not convinced. He wrote in his notebook, "Church has a case of clap" before he realized what else that could mean.

Pastor Armstrong stood and said, "The first thing we're going to do this morning is pray. We'll pray that God would control everything we say or do here today. Please bow your head and pray with me. But Adam was too busy thinking, *He cannot count. So far someone made announcements, the choir sang a special song, and a woman sang a solo. So this is at least number four, not the 'first thing.'*

Pastor Armstrong's prayer was loud and long and never mentioned God controlling everything said or done to worship him. *This man talks without thinking.*

The pastor dogmatically stated many assertions. He condemned public schools because prayer was forbidden. Adam silently wondered, *How would anyone ever know if I was praying. Just keep your eyes open, pray silently, and don't ever say 'Amen.' Just think, 'I'll talk to you again later, God.'*

He also damned public schools for denying the Bible's creation story and teaching evolution as true. Armstrong pronounced it 'evil-lewd-shun.'

Adam wondered *What does any of this have to do with knowing and trusting God?* When Armstrong said that he planned to begin a series on three crucial doctrines of the church next Sunday, Adam prepared to take notes. *Maybe I should come hear these three sermons.*

"Every genuine believer needs to hear these three sermons. If you have plans that would have you somewhere else during the next three Sundays," he said, "Change them now. Everyone who loves the Lord and this church needs to be here. If you know someone who is in the hospital, buy the DVD and give it to them—it'll reap an eternal harvest. God will bless you for it. The congregation burst into applause following each statement by Armstrong.

"The first sermon in this series will explain why water baptism is crucial for the believer." The group applauded. "Water baptism won't save a person, but a saved person will be baptized by immersion. *Applause*

"The second sermon will teach you how tithing guarantees divine financial blessings in your life." *More applause.*

"And the third sermon explains what the Bible has to say about the requirements for church membership and the command for regular attendance." The group gave Armstrong a standing ovation.

Adam wrote three words in his notebook: 'baptism, tithing, attendance.' Then he wrote, "Go to church somewhere else.' He also wrote the word *claptrap.* Later, at home, he looked up the definition and wrote *Claptrap: anything done in a way to provoke applause.*

The song leader sang a solo, and then Pastor Armstrong marched to the pulpit to preach. He said, "We are a Bible-centered church. Everything we do is based on what the Bible says the first church did. As usual, I'll be preaching from the Authorized Version of the Bible—the King James Version. The Bible our forebears read. The same Bible the founders of this great country read." During the sustained applause, Adam wondered, *I did not know that the Bible says that the first church read the King James Version of the Bible.*

"Today I want to share two passages of Scripture with you—both from the letter we call Hebrews. Some people today think they can live for God and ignore church. But the writer of Hebrews warns Christians:

> Not forsaking the assembling of ourselves together, as the manner of some is; but exhorting one another: and so much the more, as ye see the day approaching.

"Let me repeat that first part: *'Not forsaking the assembling of ourselves together, as the manner of some is…'* That's the part I want us to consider this morning. Read it for yourself in Hebrews chapter number ten and verse number five."

I'm so glad he explained that ten is a number; some of us might have thought it was a letter.

Adam's mind wandered until Rev. Armstrong raised his voice and said, "The second thing I want us to think about is holiness. We live in a day and age when people are living unholy lives like never before. People are proud of things that they should be ashamed of—a clear sign that we're in the last days. What kinds of things am I talking about? Things like sexual promiscuity and cohabitation, sexual perversions, child molestation, human trafficking and prostitution, pornography, abortion, birth control, rampant drug abuse, including prescription drugs, men with long hair and women with short hair, godless entertainment, including TV, pop music, and movies." Applause made him pause. When it ended, he said, "And I'm sure I've missed something," which provoked even more applause.

"Now let me move on to my second point. Without question God's Word declares that 'God is Holy.' On the basis of God's holiness, he commands us to be holy, because (Hebrews 12:14), 'no man shall see the Lord'. And somehow people think they can live an unholy life and still be right with God. That's a pitiful lie straight from the pit o' Hell!"

Adam had trouble paying strict attention to Armstrong's preaching. From time to time his mind wandered, only to be brought back to the message by a more strident phrase shouted louder.

Adam took notes on the sermon and wrote on his note pad:

Rev. Armstrong spoke against:

- All modern English Bible translations (he read KJV Only)
- Musical instruments in church (except piano & organ which he considered a reverent part of worship)
- Worship choruses (Armstrong called them worth-less choruses); annoyed that many church hymnals included these newer songs
- Men with long hair, beards, tattoos, piercings, & jewelry like earrings (wedding ring required on married persons)
- Women wearing pants, cutting hair, wearing makeup
- Women speaking in church
- Pop music, rock music
- Pornography, abortions, homosexuality
- Homosexuals, same-sex marriages
- Anyone who performs or who has had an abortion
- Anyone not embracing his interpretation of the Genesis creation account
- Use of tobacco, alcohol, or caffeine (as recreational drugs)
- Legalization of marijuana—including medical marijuana
- Immunizations of children for childhood diseases
- All other denominations of Christianity including Roman Catholicism and Pentecostalism
- Scientific research, especially with genetically modified organisms and stem cell research
- Birth control of any kind (even abstinence by married couples)
- Fertility research (since God opens and closes wombs)
- Public schools that forbid prayer and fail to teach the Ten Commandments
- Removal of "under God" from the Pledge of Allegiance to the US Flag
- TV and movies (as entertainment)

Three times Adam heard Armstrong say, "In conclusion," but no conclusion was forthcoming. Adam noted, "Rev. Armstrong defines the word *conclusion* differently than Mr. Webster and I do."

Later, he and Juan marveled that Armstrong could cover over twenty points in one sermon!

Loud organ music brought Adam's mind back to the church service. Diana was still sitting next to him. Adam waited until most of the crowd had left before he approached Rev. Armstrong. "Rev. Armstrong, I'm Adam Bowers, and this is Diana Norris. We're first-time visitors here."

"Welcome, Diana. Welcome Adam. We hope y'all will come back soon. Did you get a visitor's packet?"

Adam said, "No." Simultaneously Diana held up a brochure and said, "Yes, thank you."

After the obligatory questions and answers about where they live and where they work, Rev. Armstrong asked, "Can I help you in some way?"

Adam asked Rev. Armstrong his standard question, "Do you know God?"

He said, "Of course I do." Unfortunately, his tone of voice sounded arrogantly condescending.

"Please, tell me how I can know God."

He answered, "First, Stop sinning.

"Second, 'be holy as God is holy' as I preached today.

"Third, Become active in the church and grow in your faith in God. Would you like a gratis DVD of today's sermon?" But before Adam could decline the offer, Armstrong was putting one in his hands.

All Adam could say was "Thank you."

Rev. Armstrong saw someone heading toward the outside door and said, "Excuse me, Adam, pardon me Diane" and called out to a couple who seemed to be leaving without his ministerial blessing. "Doctor Watkins, just a moment. Let me greet you."

Diana corrected him, "It's Diana, not Diane," but Armstrong was to far away to hear her.

Adam saw a kiosk in the foyer and found the church covenant, which was printed on three legal-sized pieces of paper, both sides. He also picked up an application for membership in this church. Besides the usual request for name, address, phone number, previous church membership, the form also asked for the person's beliefs regarding water baptism, homosexuality, abortion, tattoos, divine inspiration of the Bible, English translations of the Bible—(especially gender-neutral translations)—evolution, prayers in public schools, and women in ministry.

Later Juan and Adam discussed Adam's experience at this church. "Adam, what did you see as positive?"

"I'm not certain this is positive, but I think it is. They venerate the Bible as divinely inspired."

"I agree, that is certainly praiseworthy."

"On the other hand, this group is just loaded with rules to follow—if not to receive God's initial forgiveness, at least to maintain right relationship with God.

"And I don't care for their dogmatism on so many issues. So for them, there's only one correct way to be baptized in water, only one acceptable Bible translation, only two musical instruments and certain old songs fitting for church worship, only certain clothes suitable for men or women to wear. Maybe I was hyper-critical of them."

"What would you prefer?"

"Maybe some humility."

"I agree with you, but I want to comment on the first thing you said about 'receiving God's forgiveness and maintaining right relationship with God.' This is the most important issue.

"In his letter to the Galatians, Paul scorches the believers for beginning a faith journey trusting in God's grace for forgiveness, and later trusting in obeying a set of rules or laws to maintain forgiveness. Paul claims that the entire faith journey is by God's grace alone. Nothing we can do will earn or maintain right standing with God. Forgiveness is always an undeserved gift."

"Wow! How did I ever come to the right conclusion about this without reading it in the Bible or you teaching me?"

"But you've read Galatians. And let's not minimize the work of God's Holy Spirit in you."

"True. I have read Galatians, but I didn't see the importance of continuing to rely on God's grace.

"Armstrong also presented faith in Christ as a panacea. Do you have financial problems? Trust Christ and he will solve your financial problems? Do you have relationship problems with a spouse or children? Trust in God to solve these problems. Cancer? God will heal you. He cited six or seven life problems like these and told us that God would solve every one. These are not his words, but it is what he preached."

Juan said, "This tendency to begin with God's grace, and switch over to maintaining relationship with God by obeying laws is what some people call 'The Galatian heresy'. At times I think it's the most common error in Evangelical Christians and Evangelical Churches.

"Presenting God as a supernatural Mr. Fix-It is another common misrepresentation of the Savior. Jesus is much more than a 'repairman.'"

"Can I just ignore God's laws? Or sin more in order to increase God's mercy and grace?"

Juan smiled as he said, "No. But our right standing with God does not depend on our following a set of rules. It depends on a living Savior. Paul addressed this in his letter to the church in Galatia."

"Juan, what does *mercy* and *grace* mean? Aren't these words synonymous—in a theological context?"

"Similar, but not identical. I'll explain it as a priest explained it to me years ago. *God's mercy* means he did not give you what you deserve, that is immediate punishment. *God's grace* means he offers you what you do not deserve, that is his forgiveness resulting in restored relationship with him."

"I think I'm full, Juan. I doubt I could learn any more today. I'll have to ponder everything we've discussed so far."

"That's okay, *mi amigo. Vaya con Dios.*" After Adam left, Juan bowed his head and whispered, "*Gracias Señor*. I do not know what you are doing in my life. But I thank you for allowing me to participate in Adam's journey to faith in Christ Jesus. God, protect him from anything wrong I've said or done. *Ser honrado en mi vida, Señor.*"

Chapter 8: Shrink Wrapped

Dr. Bailey agreed to Diana being present during their session, but he asked her to listen and say nothing unless he asked her a direct question. She agreed, and he gave her a pad of paper and a pen to jot down anything she wanted to remember to say to them.

Bailey was perplexed by what appeared to be her constant writing during the session.

He looked at Adam, "How are you processing your grief?"

"It's hard to say. I'm an emotional yo-yo. Two steps forward, one step back. I'm pretty sure my amnesia is retarding my progress—but I really don't know. I've been to work and met all my colleagues and co-workers there—they were very supportive. I'll have to get back to work sometime soon.

"The only memories I have are of Caroline. Pictures have not helped—yet, anyway. The funeral service for Caroline was much more traumatic than I thought it would be.

"Diana and I have become best friends, but we insist that she not become a replacement for Caroline."

The expression on Diana's face told Dr. Bailey that it was not 'we' insisting that, but he—and he made a note on his pad of paper.

"Diana helped me call and talk to my former wife, Sherry.

"My God-Quest is continuing. I've not found any answers yet, but I have a research plan, and I'm chipping away at it."

"So far, Adam, my contacts tell me that we have no physical evidence confirming that you were on that plane before it crashed. But if you were, I predict that empirical evidence will be forthcoming—maybe in video footage."

"I really hope it comes soon. I still have not driven a car or my motorcycle, and I'm not sure why. I probably will soon. I learned that I own a business, and…."

"A business? What kind of business?"

"Real estate. Terry Realty."

"I think I bought a house through Terry Realty years ago."

"I hope you were treated well."

"I was. The agent was tall—not as tall as you are, but heavier—with thinning, reddish-brown hair—about your age, I'd guess."

"That was probably Skip."

"I think his name was Skip."

"Not knowing how long before I'll regain my memory raises many questions in my mind. If my memory does not return, how will I run the business? Who is the best leader for the business if I have to be absent for an extended period of time? If I regain my memory, will my employees still want to work with me? What advice do you have for me, Dr. Bailey?"

"Keep doing what you're doing. Be patient, don't be too quick to trust people, don't abandon forgotten friendships, find out what music and which movies you used to like, and watch them again—if possible, with the same friends."

"Why were you anxious to have Diana with you today?"

"She's had thoughts of dying—and a few nights ago she attempted suicide."

Now Dr. Bailey turned his chair and focused his attention on Diana. "What were you writing as we talked?" She turned her pad of paper so he could see the sketch of Adam in profile.

"I had no idea that you were an artist, Diana."

"My sister was the artist. My artistic talent is minimal compared to hers."

"How are you processing your grief? Describe your process."

"Every night before I go to bed, I watch portions of a couple of home videos on DVD with Caroline in them. I have no idea if this is good for me or not. One video is my cousin's wedding—Caroline was a bridesmaid."

"Does Adam or anyone watch them with you?"

"No. I watch by myself."

"What do you do while you watch them?"

"I cry, and sometimes I talk to her—well the TV—and tell her I love her and miss her."

"Do you watch another video of her?"

"Yes. I have one taken at the lake on Adam's sailboat. I had a date and Caroline was with Adam. She got mad at Adam for throwing her in the water—'I just had my hair fixed' she shouted. He laughed and paid for her to return to the beauty salon. Only later would he learn that she told him that it cost twice what the actual price was."

Adam grinned and said, "Yeah, later she told me that."

"Let me ask another question to both of you. Do you have a strong emotional reaction over Caroline dying while you go on living?"

At the same time, they both said "Yes!"

"We call this survivor guilt. Diana, try to describe your experience with survivor guilt."

"I went to a parochial school from grades one through twelve. For years I've felt that it's wrong for a person to benefit from the death of another person. I don't know where I got this idea, other than parochial school. Four and a half years ago my Dad died, and Caroline and I each inherited over $17,500 from his estate. I felt terrible. How could I benefit from anyone's death—let alone my father's! I used the money to help pay for some of my education and to buy a better car. I felt I was honoring him by using the money this way, and so I appeased my guilt.

"This has carried over into my relationship with Adam." Adam listened intently—this was all news to him. He hoped to gain insight into his relationship with Diana.

"Ever since he and Caroline started seriously dating, I've been envious—if not jealous—of the relationship they had. He treated her so well. He was so kind, gentle, good looking, wealthy, and he even defended my honor—damn, the only thing I could find wrong with him was the fact that he was dating Caroline instead of me.

"I'm so conflicted. I want him to love me, but I also think sometimes I blame him for her death. At times I do things to make him dislike me so we won't fall in love with each other, because I believe for me to benefit from Caroline's death would be morally wrong." Adam was surprised to hear Diana's passionate description of her affection for him. This one sentence began transforming the way he viewed Diana, making his life and relationship with her even more challenging.

"And it has affected my interest in and my pursuit of Christ. I admit that I'm interested in Adam's God-Quest and Christianity. I've silently been cheering for him as he investigates its claims. And I've done a lot of personal soul searching—but how can I benefit from the death of Jesus Christ—even if it was two thousand years ago?"

"Interesting. Have you spoken to a priest or a minister about this?"

Not yet, but I'm planning to."

Now Dr. Bailey turned to Adam. "You're also suffering from survivor guilt."

He answered with passion, "Yes. I am. What was God thinking? Caroline deserved to live; I deserved to die. God must have made a mistake—if that's possible."

"Tell me about your dream. Did you ever have this dream before the plane crash?"

"Yes, I did. Maybe two or three times before the crash—and most nights since the crash. The dreams are not identical, but they are very similar with several things in common. The dream always seems so realistic, that, even when I'm awake, I'm a little uncertain that it was just a dream.

"I'm in a strange city. Sometimes I know it's Oklahoma City or Austin—other times I don't recognize which city I'm in—it could be almost anywhere. It's early afternoon, and I've checked into my hotel room a few floors up. I decide to take a brief walk—just around the block. I walk out the front door and turn right. As I begin walking, I study the buildings across the street so that I'll recognize them as I return. The road in front of my hotel is several lanes wide and filled with vehicles.

"I walk half a block and turn right. I walk a second block and turn right. I walk a third block and turn right. I walk a fourth block and turn right, and I'm sure I'm on the street the hotel is on, and it should be about half a block ahead. But, it's not there. My hotel is not there!" he shouted "I don't recognize a thing."

Adam paused long enough to become calm, then he continued, "In the dream, when I ask people for directions to that hotel, They point and tell me it's a mile away—but that's impossible—I just walked around the block, I never crossed a street, I never even crossed an alley. What universe am I in? The more I try to get to the hotel, the further away I end up."

"What do see as the common elements in this group of dreams?"

"I'm lost. Common sense that served me so well for almost thirty years is insufficient to guide me to my destination."

"Does the dream ever awaken you?"

"Yes, but not always. Even if I do not awaken, it always leaves me feeling confused and uncertain for at least an hour or two after I get up."

"Uncertain about what?"

"Pretty much everything."

"So, Diana dreams about Caroline and awakens depressed because her dream seems so much better than reality. This makes her long to join her sister in death." Dr. Bailey was looking at her, and Diana was nodding in agreement. "Diana, watching the videos may be attacking your dream time. Are you able to stop viewing it just before bedtime??"

"I think I can. I'll try."

"Adam, would you like to watch it with her?"

"She's asked me to, but I intensely do not want to watch it. But if I need to, I would try to watch it with her for her sake."

"Adam, your dreams put you in a world that you no longer comprehend and in which you cannot find your way home—or to your goal." Adam's head shook in affirmation.

"Diana, if you'd like, I'll be happy to see you as a patient by yourself. I'm very happy you came today. Adam, unless I tell you otherwise, please come see me by yourself next time. If we can schedule you two back-to-back, I can see one of you while the other one waits in the waiting room, and then you can switch places.

"Adam, no one has yet provided a satisfactory explanation for your surviving the crash. Some speculate you were not on the plane. And, frankly, I don't know what to believe. Maybe we'll find empirical, irrefutable evidence one day. Until then, I will simply believe what you say as factual. I hope you won't be offended." Adam shook his head.

Diana spoke up, "Dr. Bailey, I saw both of them board the plane and watched the plane take off."

"I understand, Diana. Please don't take offense. I'm just relaying to you the skepticism others have regarding this whole story."

After they left and went to eat lunch, Adam thought, I'm not sure I want to describe what I experienced when God rescued me from the plane. Maybe I will if we get physical evidence that convinces everyone that I was on that plane.

Chapter 9: A Step of Faith

Skip and Adam had ridden together from Terry Realty to a ritzy restaurant and were now seated in a small private room. At first the conversation centered on small talk. Adam began the dialogue. "Where'd you get the nickname 'Skip'?"

"It was the only brand of peanut butter I'd eat as a kid. My father started calling me Skip—and it stuck."

"I guess that's better than being called 'Jif'."

"Not much. Adam, do you remember when and where we first met?"

"You know I don't. Tell me."

"We were both students at UT. I was majoring in business and minoring in advertising; you were majoring in accounting and minoring in business. We weren't roommates, but we lived on the same floor of a men's dorm."

"So we had some business classes together?"

"No. We were officers in the UT Atheists Club. We were campus spokesmen for atheism. We talked about minoring in philosophy of science."

"Really? Why?"

"We thought the course would support our atheism."

"Once years ago you asked me if I could imagine anything that could possibly cause me to abandon atheism and embrace theism, like philosopher Anthony Flew did years ago. We both thought about it long and hard, and discussed it from time to time.

"About this same time you asked me, 'What would you think if God appeared to you in a vision?' I replied, 'I'd assume I'd hallucinated'."

"You said, 'Even though you'd never hallucinated before in your life, you'd never used hallucinogens, and you could not possibly have a 'flash-back'—since you never had a 'flash' at all?

"We boasted that our god was science. We claimed that the energy and matter of the universe is all that exists. We were empiricists who believed only in things detectable by the physical senses. We denied everything supernatural.

"We once challenged a Christian to admit that theoretically Christianity could be falsified if the bones of Jesus of Nazareth were found. He responded by asking us if the verification principle could verify itself and could the falsification principle be falsified in any empirical way. We all three laughed and became friends. He stayed a Christian, and we remained atheists. He vowed that he would never stop praying for us."

"Okay." Pause. "Why are you telling me this, Skip?"

"Diana told me that you claim God rescued you from the plane crash, and that you're trying to find a way to 'know God'. Do you want to tell me about it?"

"Very much, but not now. I will tell you one day. Later. I think I need to regain my memory first."

"Years ago, I would have been the first and only person to whom you spoke about this. Are you exploring other religions like Buddhism and Hinduism, or just Christianity?"

"Just different brands of Christianity at first. Maybe I'll evaluate Buddhism or Hinduism more later. I've read enough about those two to lose interest in them."

"But these religions are older and have more adherents than Christianity, too."

"I know, but truth is not determined by a majority vote or how long people have believed something, Skip. And Christianity is the only religion I know that is at least coherent with my experience—the others are not."

By this time, they had finished eating, and Skip produced two cigars from his sport coat inside pocket. "We would sometime smoke a good cigar after a business meeting. I brought two. D'you want one?"

"Sure. Thanks. Do I smoke?"

"Maybe two or three cigars a year, nothing else. They're Cuban. Cohiba." Adam did not recall how to smoke a cigar, so he watched everything Skip did and mimicked it. After they had the cigars fired up, the discussion continued.

"Okay. How will you know if Christianity is true? How can its claims be objectively verified or objectively falsified?"

"I'm not sure yet. Maybe they can only be subjectively verified or subjectively falsified. But I think you have a couple of other questions we should talk about first."

"Like what?"

"No, Skip. Please, ask me the real questions on your mind—don't hesitate. I insist. You fear you don't know who I am—with good reason—I don't know who I am. But, trust me, I'm still your friend. If I have a hidden agenda, I have no idea what it is—it's also hidden from me. What's the real question or questions on your mind?"

"Okay. You're right. You're as brilliant as you always were as a student at UT. I have two questions about our future at Terry Realtors. First question: If you became a theist or a Christian, would our working relationship change because I'm still an atheist? Can a Christian and an atheist be friends and business partners?"

"Wow. Those questions never even crossed my mind. So my first reply is 'Yes!' And I really believe that, and hope I'm not mistaken. I know so little about God and Christianity that I admit I could be wrong.

"Let's assume for this discussion that I become a Christian. Our business arrangements were solidified long before my conversion. As a Christian, I would guess I'd still be bound by our written and verbal contracts. Or we'd have to reach a mutually satisfactory dissolution of those contracts. In any event, you're my friend regardless of your religious convictions or your political party. And you own ten percent of the TR stock."

"Eleven percent, and soon to be twelve percent. Each year I earn another percent until I own twenty percent—at which point it's capped." Skip smiled and said, "It's true. Your facial expression says you don't remember that, but it's in the minutes of the meeting of the board, so I'm not concerned. Do you remember that Sherry owns five percent of the company? She provided most of the money we needed for start-up years ago."

"Yeah, I knew that she owned five percent, but I thought it was part of the divorce settlement."

"Nope. She provided the start-up capital."

"Do I need to put it in writing that you cannot be terminated because of your faith—or lack of faith—in God?"

"I don't think so. We'll see."

"What's your second question?"

"If you become a theist or a Christian, will I still want to work with you? I don't know the answer to that question. I've never worked with a

Christian—oh I've worked with people who said they were Christians and went to church every Sunday, but I've never worked with anyone who even lived up to half of what Christians supposedly believe. I have no basis for having a colleague and friend who's a Christian, and I admit that it makes me nervous. Changes in your life will definitely affect me, friend."

"Skip, are all TR employees atheists? Or are some deists? Are some Christians? Or Buddhists? Or something else? Does TR collect that data?"

"We never have, and I have no idea of the religious beliefs or political convictions of anyone who works at TR. I think Tina or Jackie is some kind of a Christian, but I could be wrong.

"Adam, we've had two hard fast rules for employees since Day One: first, keep your religious convictions to yourself, and second, keep your political persuasion to yourself. Employees are asked not to have religious decals or political signs on their cars or in their yards. We told them, 'We don't care what you are, but you must not let those interfere with your work.' In ten years, we've never had a problem with either one. I don't even know if any of them go to church or vote."

"How close are you to abandoning your atheism?"

"I don't know. All I can say right now is this: If I was doing something and I found out God did not want me to, I'd quit.

"Well, thanks for bringing your thoughts to me, Skip. And I hope you'll always be this candid and forthright with me."

"I probably can't be any other way. I hope you will always be this charitable. My hope for you is that you will avoid the 'divine delusion.' So when are you going to tell me what happened?"

"Later. It's time for you to get back to work and earn us some money."

"Great. The Boss is back."

While riding back to the office, Adam said, "Skip, tell me about the lawsuit."

"There's not much to tell, really. Our attorneys assure us that we'll win.

"We're fighting to keep our membership in the National Association of Realtors. One of our former clients claims that we bribed an appraiser to inflate the value of property. The lawsuit names us and the appraiser, Pete Pierce. If we lose the lawsuit, the NRA will probably revoke our membership and TR will no longer be able to use the label Realtor."

"Are we guilty?"

"Our attorneys assure us that we'll win. The suit may even be dismissed."

"How can our lawyers make that claim? On what basis?"

"The plaintiffs don't have the evidence to prove their claim."

"Again, are we guilty? Did we bribe an appraiser?"

"You didn't." Before Adam could rephrase his question, Skip continued, "Adam, if you were to regain your memory, would you still be on a quest to know God?"

"I guess so. The quest is really to learn how I was saved from certain death, and why I was saved. Both 'how' and 'why'."

Skip said, "Adam, there just has to be a natural explanation."

"Give me a credible natural explanation for falling from thirty thousand feet to the ground without a parachute and landing uninjured. Why must everything have a *natural explanation*? Is it just because we embrace the presupposition that there is no such thing as the *supernatural?*"

"Because science has shown us that there is a natural explanation for everything."

"Everything Skip? How do you know that? Your statement is not a scientific statement, it's a philosophical assumption."

"I know, but it's true. You cannot refute my argument, Adam."

"Just the opposite: A man with an experience is never at the mercy of a man with an argument, Skip. You cannot refute my experience."

"But few people have ever claimed to have had the experience you have claimed to have had with God."

"God has convinced countless thousands of people in essentially every country that he exists. Back to the question of the business—I suspect that if I became a Christian like my friend Juan, I'd probably want to operate TR with God as the CEO."

Skip thought he was being humorous as he said, "Would God be present at meetings of the board?"

"Probably, even if we didn't see or hear him. To say it another way, I would probably want to operate TR on godly, New Testament principles. Like Jesus taught in what we call 'The Golden Rule'."

"You mean 'Do unto others as you would have them do to you'? Adam, the NAR's ethical demands are tough enough, don't you think? We'll never make money that way."

"I don't even know if anything we do is on the border of *unethical.*"

"Trust me, Adam. We don't. Never have. Never will." After they stood and were walking out the door, Skip said, "Adam, if you become a Christian, what will you do about Kevin?"

"Who's Keven?"

"TR's newest junior salesman?"

"What d'you mean, what would I do about him?"

"He's homosexual."

"Oh, did I know that when we hired him?"

"Yes."

"Has he been annoying clients with his sexual preferences?"

"To my knowledge, no."

"If he is obnoxious with his sexuality, I guess we'd warn him first and fire him second—just as we would a heterosexual who is obnoxious about his or her sexual preference. Is there a bigger problem that I don't know about?"

"None I know of. And I agree with your statement regarding a heterosexual."

"Who usually hires and fires sales people?"

"I do."

"Then I guess I'd ask you what you plan to do about Kevin."

"I'll remind you of that one day, if I need to. As CEO, you have veto power."

"Oh. Right."

Chapter 10: Faith Crisis

Adam recognized that the more time he spent with Diana, the more attractive she was becoming to him. Even though his personal beliefs and convictions had not developed to the point of his thinking sexual intercourse outside of marriage was wrong, he did think that a sexual relationship with her at this time would be both dishonest and destructive. This prompted Adam to tell her, "Diana, I cannot sleep over at your apartment anymore."

"Why not? We haven't even come close to having sex. We have never even kissed, and the only time you hugged me, you hugged me as you would a girl of ten. Did I do something wrong?"

"No. In a nutshell, I'm too attracted to you. I don't want to have to struggle against my sex drive—or yours. I think I should plan to spend the night in my own home from now on."

"I'd be lying if I told you that this makes me happy. I cannot label my feelings for you, but I like you very much, and I don't want us to stop seeing each other."

"Well, I don't want to stop seeing you either. I just don't want the stimulation of being alone with you in the apartment for long periods of time."

Adam had no idea that he had just made a decision that would help him to avoid temptation—it was a milestone.

"Don't just leave it at that, Adam. Tell me what you have in mind, and let me express my opinions too."

"Okay. If you agree, I'd like for you to continue visiting churches with me when I visit them on Sunday mornings."

"Good. I'd like that."

"I'd like for you to continue going with me when I see Juan and Esperanza on Tuesday evenings."

"Thanks for inviting me—I'd like to do that too. Esperanza and I are becoming close friends."

"Maybe we could go ice skating or roller skating two or three times a month."

With laughter she replied, "Nope. You're on your own there my friend. Falling on your rear end just makes it get bigger."

"Just seeing if you were paying attention. You told me that I liked to line dance, but I'm not sure I remember that. I probably need the exercise, and Dr. Bailey said it might help me regain memory. He also said I should minimize consumption of alcoholic beverages."

"I'll try line dancing, but I've never been a fan. Do you want me to curtail drinking too?"

"Could you?"

"Probably. At least for a while—or when I'm around you."

"And we could eat together every Friday or Saturday night."

"Not 'or,' Friday **and** Saturday night. Real food. Not fast food."

"So noted."

"Bowling?"

"No."

"Miniature golf?"

"No."

"Bungee jumping?"

"No thanks."

"Good. Skydiving?"

Diana mimicked Adam, "Hay-Yil no!"

"Good. You have other ideas, just tell me."

"Okay. We could do something on Sunday evenings too."

"So noted."

"I also like hiking, sailing, water skiing, and going to movies."

"All right. I'm glad we got this all straightened out. I'm going home now. Good night, M'Lady."

Diana slept peacefully because she'd noticed that instead of calling her "Kiddo," he had called her "M'Lady"—for the first time.

At Panera that Tuesday evening, Juan said, "One of the things you should keep in mind, Adam, is that God designed and created us humans in his image for a reason, a purpose."

"And that is…?"

"To have fellowship with him and with other humans. We were not designed to be recluses but to live in intimate friendship with him and with people. That's not his only reason for creating us, but that's the foundation.

"Consider anything designed and manufactured by humans. One tool was designed to open metal cans, another was designed to cut meat, and another was designed to take pictures. If you try to take a picture with a can opener, your friends will think you're not too bright. If you try to open a can of beans with your camera, you probably won't be too successful— and you might damage the camera.

"God designed us to live in relationship with him and others. We can achieve our maximum potential only as we foster those relationships— instead of attempting to control our own lives. We have to learn to submit ourselves to God's rulership."

"You think I should have no part in deciding what I do, where I go, what I say?"

"No, that's not what I'm saying. God has given us a free will, but he wants us to choose to live a life consistent with his nature and with his will. God want us to live, but to let him control our words and actions."

"How long will it take me to become a perfect Christian, like you, Juan?"

Juan smiled, "All of your life on earth—and more. I'm not even close to perfect—and neither is any other believer on the face of this earth. Adam, Perfection is not the distinguishing characteristic of a Christian."

"It's not? What's the mark then?"

"The Bible tells us that genuine Christians will demonstrate the love of Christ to people—believers and non-believers. And when this life is over, God will change us into perfection."

"It's much easier to say, 'Demonstrate the love of Christ to people— believer and non-believer'—than it is to do it."

"True. That takes the power of God's Holy Spirit in a person."

Chapter 11: Breakdown Near Maypearl

One morning while Adam was riding his Harley in the countryside south of Dallas and near Waxahachie, the drive belt on his bike broke, stranding him in the country between Italy and Maypearl, not far from the Interstate.

Adam spoke to the belt, "I don't remember when you should have been replaced, but surely it was before today. Now what do I do?" First he pulled out his cell phone and called Diana, but all he heard was a message telling him that she would be in class until she went to work.

Then he remembered Juan had told him that God cares about the small problems of life as well as the big ones. He put his cell phone back in his pocket, bowed his head, and said, "God, please send someone to help me."

He returned to look at the broken belt. As he was considering his options, another biker came by and stopped to help him. Adam was too relieved to be nervous. A large man walked over to him, held out his hand, and said, "Hi. I'm Frank. Can I help you?"

"Thanks, Frank. I'm Adam. My drive belt broke." He pointed to it as he spoke.

"I have the tools and know how to replace it here if you have a new belt. Do you have a replacement in the saddlebags?"

"I don't know—and I haven't looked." They looked, but no replacement belt was found.

"I could take you the nearest Harley dealer to get another, if you'd like."

"That would be awesome. Thanks." The two of them pushed Adam's Harley where it would be out of the road and not obvious to every passer-by. Then Frank turned his bike around and started it. Adam climbed behind Frank, and they headed into town.

Frank obviously knew his way around town, and in about 20 minutes, they pulled into a motorcycle repair shop on the eastern edge of Waxahachie. Adam bought the belt, and they headed back.

While they were working to replace the belt, Adam told Frank about his amnesia and his business in Plano. "Sure, I know where Terry Realty is— it's not far from where I work."

"Where do you work, Frank?"

"I'm the pastor at Biblical Community Church in northeastern Ft. Worth."

"You don't look like a minister, Frank."

"Thank you. Let me return the compliment. You don't look like a Realtor. What do you think a pastor looks like?"

"Well, the Harley is atypical, and your tattoos are not typical either—unless they're a part of your denomination, which I would not know. Are they?"

"No, but there's a story behind the tattoos."

"Tell it to me."

"A few years ago, we had a young man whose parents went to our church. I'd prayed with the parents two or three times for their 19-year-old son. He was an art major in college, and he was using recreational drugs, regularly drinking to excess, and was sexually promiscuous.

"One Sunday this young man had a life-changing experience with God. Over the next several weeks we watched and were amazed at how dramatically God was turning his life right-side-up. Many people in the church were encouraged to see his faithful commitment to the Lord Jesus Christ.

"Then some of the older saints in the church asked him, 'Gabe, what d'you think God wants to do with you? Do you have any idea what God has called you to do?'

"Gabe was extremely talented artistically, and he did not hesitate to reply, 'God has called me to be the best tattoo artist in the world.'

"Some of these older saints were stunned and upset by his reply. 'Oh, no,' they told him, 'You cannot be a Christian and a tattoo artist'.

"When I heard this, I was angry and annoyed. I wanted to affirm Gabe in his faith, so when I saw him I told him, 'Gabe, don't let these older Christians bother you. Just trust and serve God, and allow God to lead, guide, and direct you.

"He grinned and told me, 'Don't worry Rev, they don't bother me—I ignore them. Really, I don't even listen to them.'

"That evening I was feeling real good about affirming Gabe in his new-found faith, and this thought came to my mind—I don't know if God put it there or not: *that's not how you affirm Gabe in his faith—if you want to affirm Gabe in his faith, ask him, 'Gabe, can you give me a tattoo?* Never in my life have I ever considered getting a tattoo. Never."

Adam laughed out loud and said, "Really?"

"Yes. It happened exactly as I'm telling it. I looked for several months before I found an image that I thought would honor God." Frank turned to show Adam the upper part of his left arm. "Some people claim that the oldest artist's conception of Jesus is similar to this: Jesus as the Good Shepherd carrying the lost lamb. I am that lost lamb.

"Less than a year later, I emailed Gabe and asked him, 'What do you think about this image for the upper part of my right arm?' Then Frank showed him the tattoo on his other arm: an image of Jesus washing Peter's feet. "Gabe answered, 'Let's do it'."

"Very artistic. Great shading too. What do the people at your church think of these tattoos?"

"I'm sure some of them cling to the old traditions and still think that good people don't have tattoos. But the younger people really like them. If I had known how useful they would be in opening the door for me to witness to people, I would've gotten them years ago."

Adam said, "Tell me about Biblical Community Church."

Frank said, "I'd love to. We're non-denominational."

"Does that mean your members don't believe anything?"

"No. Maybe that's why some of them prefer to say we're 'trans-denominational'."

"That means members can believe anything?"

Frank grinned and said, "No. Tell you what, wise-guy, I'll tell you what we believe, and you tell me what words communicate that idea."

Adam laughed, "Okay. I'll try."

"We have very strong convictions about Jesus of Nazareth: his life, his teaching, and his divinity, about the Bible, and about God's offer of forgiveness to humans.

"On many other issues, we allow believers to hold differing opinions and convictions, and we encourage them not to fight with other believers over those doctrines. So, for example, some are Calvinists and others are Arminians."

"What does that mean?"

"Some believe God has chosen who will trust him, while others think that people have a free will and must choose to accept or reject God's offer of forgiveness."

"Oh, okay. Which one should I believe?"

"I really don't care. Some of our members think Christians should abstain from all alcohol, while others drink beer or wine. Some are Pentecostal, others are non-Pentecostal. Some come to church in shorts, others wear suits and ties. Some women wear makeup and jewelry, others wear neither. Some members are premillennialists, some are postmillennialists, and others are amillennialists. Some of our members are young earth creationists, some are progressive creationists, others are evolutionary creationists, and some others are apathetic on the topic.

"BCC has four professional ministers: I'm the senior pastor or lead pastor. We have a pastor to the children, to the youth, and to senior citizens. The Church Board of Trustees is made up of the pastor and eleven people, four of whom are women. The Board of Deacons has both men and women.

"We have Anglos, Latinos, African-Americans, and Indigenous Americans—all of whom participate in every aspect of church life: the choir, orchestra, teachers, ushers, deacon board, trustee board, housekeeping, and nursery workers.

"So what label communicates those ideas?"

"I can't do any better than 'Biblical Community Church.' Tell me about the church's 'strong convictions,' please."

"Sure. Generally these four big areas: Scripture, Jesus, humanity, and the church—and how these relate to the message of the Gospel.

"First, the Bible is seen as the authority in what we teach and how we live."

"A particular translation of the Bible?"

"No. We use several English translations. Some of the older people still like the KJV, but I usually use one of more modern English translations in teaching and preaching.

"Second, Jesus of Nazareth is considered uniquely divine and the Messiah God promised to the Jews. So we believe what the Bible tells us about Jesus, about humans, and about God's offer of forgiveness.

"Third, God will punish humans who reject his offer of forgiveness through the atoning substitutionary death of Christ Jesus on the cross. There is a real Heaven to be gained and a real Hell to be avoided.

"And fourth, if there is a fourth—has to do with the Church, that group of people committed to believing and obeying God. The Church is part of God's plan to proclaim forgiveness to sinners and to live a Christ-like life in this world."

"Rev. Noble, Do you know God?"

"I'm sure you know my answer is yes."

"Tell me how I can know God."

"Adam, I think God has already revealed himself to you. Am I right?"

"Yes."

"So you do know him."

"Well, I met Nicholas Cage once, but I couldn't truthfully say that I know him."

"So, what are you searching for? Do you want a right relationship with God?"

"Yeah. I think that's what I want. Thanks for helping me articulate it better."

"The Bible reveals only one right relationship of humans with God, and that's with God being the Boss, Lord, Master, and Ruler, and the human being the obedient slave or servant. With this in mind, a typical sequence is this: First, a person grasps his or her sinful condition and confesses these sins to God.

"This motivates that person to trust in the substitutionary death of Christ on the cross as payment for his/her sins. God responds by changing that person in a way that Jesus compared to being 'born again.'

"As this reborn person learns more God's nature and what Christ has done for us, he or she pledges himself/herself to working with God's Spirit in developing the character traits of Jesus in his/her life."

"Adam, how would you describe where you are in your journey to faith in Christ?"

"I'm not really sure. But as you were describing those, uh…features of coming to know God, I was silently affirming each one in prayer."

"So you would say that you have been reborn?"

"No. I'd probably say that I'm in the process of being reborn. Is that okay?"

"I think it's far beyond 'okay'. I'm confident God will continue to bring you to faith him."

"My late fiancée's sister, Diana, and I are visiting churches in the DFW Metroplex. We'll have to plan to visit Biblical Community Church sometime soon."

"I hope you will. We have a group of bikers who take day-trips and weekend trips from time to time. Maybe you'll ride with us sometime."

"Thanks. I might take you up on that." The two men swapped business cards, cell phone numbers, and email addresses, and Frank and Adam rode off in separate directions.

Later Adam called Juan and said, "I had a real interesting experience today. Can we meet later and talk about it?"

"Sure. Why don't you and Diana come over after dinner, and we'll talk then?"

"Okay. We'll be there between 6:30 and 7:00. Would you like for me to bring something?"

""Yes, bring Diana and no alcohol."

During the drive to Juan's, Diana pestered Adam, "Tell me about your experience today."

All Adam would tell her was, "No, I don't want to tell the story twice—be patient, you can hear it when I tell Juan and Esperanza." They expected to see Esperanza there with Juan, and they were not surprised.

After the initial pleasantries and hugs, they sat around a circular table, drinking coffee and eating slices of rhubarb-strawberry pie with generous scoops of vanilla ice cream that Esperanza had just cooked. She said, "So, tell us what happened to you today, Adam."

"I was riding my Harley out in the country west of Waxahachie—near Maypearl—when the drive belt broke. I was stranded. I tried to reach Diana on the cell phone, but got no answer—just a recording. I prayed and asked God for help. In less than five minutes, another motorcyclist came along, stopped, and offered to help me. We rode on his bike to a dealer and I bought a new drive belt. He took me back to my bike and helped me install it."

"So far, not too exciting or interesting."

"Only then did I discover that his name was Frank Noble, and he's the pastor of Biblical Community Church. Juan, do you know Rev. Noble?"

Juan laughed, "Yes, I do. He's a character isn't he? And I have worshiped at Biblical Community Church several times."

"So how would you describe that church?"

"Here's how I would describe it, from my limited observation as a non-member," Juan said. "BCC seems to be Christ-centered and Bible-based; it's fresh, modern, and accepting."

"What do you mean by 'accepting'?"

"The people who worship there don't argue over personal convictions or peripheral doctrines—they focus on the teachings of Jesus and trust God's Spirit to lead individuals. They don't really care if you are a Dispensationalist or a Covenantalist, a Pentecostal or a non-Pentecostal, a Calvinist or an Arminian.

"They have a reputation of loving people—even sinners, bad people. And the pastor has a nickname—many people purposely mispronounce the name Noble as No Bull, because he doesn't mince words. He preaches in a candid and conversational style and makes applications to everyday life.

"Very few people dress up on Sunday morning; women rarely wear dresses; some room is left for individuals to have different convictions. Noble is probably one of the few ministers in Texas who has a functioning Board of Elders instead of a group of men and women who just rubber-stamp whatever he says."

Adam asked Juan, "Did you see anything that you thought was a weakness? At BCC?"

"Maybe. I'm not sure. I think these are all things that you taught me. At times they seemed to worship the Bible—Jesus died for our sins, not the Bible.

"Some of them seem to forget that the autographs were divinely inspired, not modern translations or modern interpretations. And they seem to ignore the role of the Holy Spirit in sanctification. Sometimes they sound like sanctification depends entirely on the Christian."

"Three good observations, Adam. But you may be pre-judging them. Be careful. One day you may be the very Christian that you are evaluating today."

Later, after Adam and Diana attended Biblical Community Church, Juan asked him again to describe their experience. "In many ways, I like the way Noble preaches. It includes a lot of teaching. But he preached from the Old Testament, the book of Daniel, and he hardly mentioned Jesus Christ. I don't recall hearing anything about Christians caring for the poor, the hungry, or the homeless at BCC."

"Give him time, Adam, you've only heard him preach once. He doesn't pack twenty points into one sermon, the way some preachers do."

All Diana would say is, "I liked it. I want to go back there sometime. We don't know any of the songs they sang, but I liked the music, and I can learn the songs."

Chapter 12: Humanism

Diana asked, "Adam, do you remember that you're a humanist—a secular humanist?"

"What's that mean?"

Diana said, "I'm not sure how to define humanism, Adam. So I'll read a quote from a recent copy of the AHA magazine.

Humanism is a progressive philosophy of life that, without theism and other supernatural beliefs, affirms our ability and responsibility to lead ethical lives of personal fulfillment that aspire to the greater good of humanity.

"Apparently their slogan is *Good Without A God.* They deny the existence of anything supernatural, thus denying every form of theism. Interesting. I know you were an atheist, Adam, but you were very kind to Caroline and me."

"Are you an atheist, Diana?"

"Me? No, I went to parochial school, which did seem to drive one or two kids toward atheism—but not me."

Later, Juan asked Adam, "What do you see as the strengths and weaknesses of the teachings and practices of humanism?"

"In my opinion, this group has more weaknesses than strengths.

"First, they deny the existence of God, which is contrary to my experience. And a person with an experience is never at the mercy of a person with an argument."

Juan said, "They've removed God from the position of *Supreme Being* and elevated humans and human reasoning to the status of *Supreme Being.*

Once, when Juan was visiting Adam at Terry Realty, Adam asked him, "Juan, why do you think we have so many Christian denominations?"

"I'm not the first to try to answer that question. Some people see denominations as a splintered church—an ungodly and fragmented body of Christ—and they could be right. But it could also indicate that Christians may take slightly different roads on their journeys.

"Maybe this single example will help illustrate this: One major difference in denominations is in their church government. Gordon Fee points out in his commentary on the Pastoral Epistles that virtually all Christian denominations point to the same passages in the same books of the Bible as their authority for 'biblical Church government'—and yet the churches in these different denominations have very different forms of ecclesiastical government.

"He comments that if the Apostle Paul intended for the Pastoral Epistles to be a church manual, he did not entirely succeed. He argues that Timothy in Ephesus and Titus in Crete should be seen less as pastors of a church than as Paul's apostolic representative to that church."

Another day, when Skip and Adam were working on a plan for a TV advertisement, Tina interrupted them. Tina opened the door of Adam's office enough to show her face and said, "Mr. Bowers, a Mr. Juan Reyes is here to see you."

"Thanks, Tina. Bring him in. Don't leave, Skip, I want you to meet Juan."

"Come in Juan. This is one of my best friends and business associate, Michael Masters—but we all call him Skip. Skip, this is my close friend and spiritual mentor, Juan Reyes."

Juan and Skip shook hands and said, "Nice to meet you." But Adam sensed the immediate tension between the two men.

Skip began the discussion, "So you're the man trying to convert my atheist buddy to Christianity."

Juan smiled, "Yes, I am. And you're Adam's atheist friend who thinks *religion* and *philosophy* are two separate non-overlapping categories. Skip, I've heard a little about the long friendship you two have shared—mostly from Diana Norris. I'm glad to finally meet you."

With a condescending tone, Skip said, "I guess the fundamental difference between philosophy and religion is that religion requires faith, while philosophy does not."

Juan ignored Skip's condescending tone, and he did not hesitate to participate in this exchange, "Many people acknowledge that philosophers have faith in their methods and in human reason to answer all questions."

Skip continued, "Religion uses polite language that lacks criticism, while in philosophy, the language used is meant to help a person to discover the truth—and criticisms are very likely there. "

"Sorry to disagree again, but your statement reveals you don't read religion or theology journals. There is much criticism, sometimes polite, other times not so much, and its purpose is also to discover truth."

Skip countered, "In religion people gain knowledge through revelation from a supernatural person or realm, and truth is communicated through faith and authority. In philosophy knowledge is gained through conversation, reasoning, and thinking."

'Skip, as I already pointed out, philosophers also have and use faith— but it is faith in themselves, their rationality and reasoning, and in human ability. Surely you will acknowledge some philosophers are considered authoritative."

Skip was unrelenting, "The difference is how you reach the truth. Religion relies on belief in what you perceive as coming from the Divine. Philosophy relies on human reason and logic."

"I think we're getting close now, Skip. True, religion often claims a divine deity, but Buddhism is usually classified as *religion*, and it does not identify deity. Atheists deny God exists and that he alone occupies a position of *Supreme Being*, and they typically posit that humans are in that lofty position. Some even admit that atheism functions as a godless religion.

"Both philosophers and Christians use reason and logic. But Christians recognize the God of the Bible as *Supreme Being* and humans as created beings. I guess it is possible to re-define religion and philosophy so they are different. But are they really different? Or just two sides of one piece of paper? You see atheism as your conclusion; I think it's your top starting presupposition. If you'd like, we could continue this conversation another time."

Had Skip stated the thought in his mind—*This man is not your average migrant worker*—his bigotry would have been obvious. As it was, he wisely kept it hidden.

Adam and Juan had no idea of the effect of Juan's words were having on Skip Masters. Skip was too annoyed to notice, as well.

Chapter 13: A Hasty Wedding

"Diana, get ready—we're going to a wedding!"

'What? Where? I'm not dressed for a wedding. My hair's a mess. And I'm supposed to meet my study group. Where are you? Who's getting married?"

"You don't have to get dressed up. Forget your study group meeting this once. Juan and Esperanza are getting married in less than an hour, and they want us to be there. No one is invited except both families and us. I'll be there in ten minutes to pick you up, so get ready."

Diane was ready and waiting, but mildly apprehensive. She opened the driver's door and pushed Adam over so she could drive.

"I doubt Juan wants me at his wedding, Adam."

"He told me to get you and get to the church. He said they'd wait until we're there before he lets them start."

As they rode toward the church in Frisco. Diana asked, "I thought they were getting married late next month. Why'd they move it up?"

"I don't know, but we can guess, huh?"

"D'you think Juan just couldn't control his sex drive? Is she pregnant? I bet he knocked her up." She laughed at the idea of Juan failing this way.

"I don't know either, but I'd say that's a pretty safe guess."

Her tone of voice changed when she said, "So a year ago he was too holy to sleep with me, and now he can't wait another four or five weeks to jump her bones? I guess that's the only logical explanation. She is very attractive—and sexy too."

"I'm sure you're probably right."

Esperanza wore a beautiful white wedding gown. Both of her parents, one on her left and one on her right, walked her to the front of the sanctuary where Juan, wearing a new dark suit and tie, waited for her with his brothers. Not counting the wedding party, about two dozen family members were present. Most of the ceremony was in Spanish, but the priest was bilingual and restated most of it in English for Adam and Diana.

During the actual ceremony, Diana leaned over to Adam and said, "Why is everyone crying?"

"Many people cry at weddings, Diana. Strong emotion, even joyful emotions, cause some people to cry."

"I know that, but everyone cries without some breaks to breathe. All of their family members are crying, and some of these people have never stopped. This is strange. Maybe it's a Hispanic custom."

"I doubt it. But I don't know. Now, Shh!"

The ceremony was short and to the point. Several people moved around the room taking flash pictures, and one girl walked around with a new Sony digital video camera on a tripod. The flash from the cameras did not seem to distract the priest, Juan, or Esperanza. Almost everything emphasized the festive atmosphere—everything except members of both families constantly wiping away their tears.

After the ceremony, the group moved into a smaller room for a reception of cake, punch, nuts, and pictures. During the ceremony and reception, Espereanza's brother, Eduardo, took many photos with a digital SLR and posted them on Facebook.

Diana was trying to see if Esperanza's abdomen had a 'baby bump,' but she detected nothing. She wanted to ask her if she was expecting, but she didn't dare ask with her family in hearing range.

Esperanza surprised everyone when she said, "Diana, would you please go with me into the next room and help me change from my wedding gown into my travel clothes?"

"Sure. Glad to help." And she thought, *Now that's strange. Why didn't she ask her mother or sister to help her?* It never crossed her mind that Esperanza was telling her 'You're a special friend to me, Diana.'

Now's my chance, Diana thought as she unbuttoned the back of the wedding gown. "Esperanza, why did you and Juan get married today? Were you in a hurry for the honeymoon?"

"No. We won't have a honeymoon. We're going to a Super 8 or a Motel 6 near the airport. I will tell you the rest, but you must promise to tell no one, or Juan will be very angry with me."

Here it comes, she thought. *She's pregnant, and they don't want anyone to know.*

"I would never tell anyone. I promise." Then before Esperanza could explain, Diana said, "You're pregnant, aren't you?"

"What? No, I'm not pregnant! Juan and I are still virgins anxiously anticipating the consummation of our marriage tonight." Her facial expression and tone of voice mirrored her indignation at this suggestion of pre-marital sex. "God has helped us to control our sexual desires for each other. With God as my witness, we have been faithful to God and to each other."

Diana frowned, "Get out! If you're not pregnant, why'd you have this quickie wedding?"

"Please, don't let Juan know that I told you. You must keep it *secreto!* Promise?"

"I promise."

Tears filled her eyes as she said, "Juan has inoperable cancer. The doctors say he will probably live only four to six more weeks! Our families know, but he wants to work as long as he has strength. I'm hoping that I will get pregnant before he dies."

A flood of embarrassment swept over Diana. *Damn. That really sucks. Juan is the most Christian person I've ever known. Why doesn't God do something about this?* Her face reflected her thoughts, and Esperanza noticed it.

"Diana, I do not know why God allows this. But I'm sure that God can and will heal his cancer—if it fits his will and purpose for us. And, I pray you will one day find this faith and trust in God too, Diana."

She thought, *Yeah, well I'm not sure if I want to trust a God who thinks dying of cancer is okay.*

"You're one of my favorite people in the whole world, Diana."

Diana was shocked by this expression of affection, but she recovered quickly and said, "And I love you, Esperanza," and they sealed their mutual affection with an embrace. The wedding party applauded as Esperanza rejoined them at the reception.

Diana walked over and stood by Adam. In a moment, she whispered, "Adam, they have no money for a honeymoon. They're just going to a cheap motel near the airport for a day or two, and then to Esperanza's apartment. They plan to live there until he...uh, I mean, well, for a few weeks maybe." Adam caught her intended meaning without her saying it.

"No!" Adam walked outside and called someone on his cell phone. "Hi Jackie, this is Adam Bowers. Do we use a travel agent for TR? Chris? Great. Please send his name and number as a text to my cell phone. Her name, right. Thanks." Two minutes later his cell phone signaled a text had arrived. He opened it and copied the name and number into his pocket notepad.

In another minute he said, "Chris? Yes, this is Adam Bowers. According to my notes, you're my travel agent, right?

"Except for memory problems, I'm doing great, thank you. I need you to help me. This is a rush—I need to finish this in 15 minutes—20 minutes max. Let me know if you think you can do this, please. Thanks. I need you to buy two tickets to fly from D/FW airport to Bermuda.

"No. Not for me. Their names are Juan and Esperanza Reyes. So you need me to spell the names?

"Also, book hotel reservations at a fancy upscale hotel for them.

"Yes, on the ocean. Do you think you can do that? I'm not sure when or how I'll pay for it.

"Oh, yes, please use Terry Realtors' credit card to pay for all of it.

"Yes. Just call me back with the details. I look forward to meeting you sometime.

"Oh, I have met you. Yes, I certainly should remember that. Call me back if you have any problem. Thank you."

Adam never knew that Chris immediately called Tina to confirm that she should follow Adam's instructions. But since Chris never told Tina that the tickets and hotel room were for Mr. and Mrs. Juan Reyes, Tina wrongly concluded that Adam had suddenly married—probably Diana. And since Tina was the self-appointed office public relations officer—also known as the office gossip—she made a point of telling Chris about Caroline's death and Adam's amnesia, but she said "good-bye" and hung up the phone before Chris could tell her that the tickets were not for Adam and Diana.

A minute later Adam was back in the church with the wedding party. No one noticed his absence. Sixteen minutes later his cell rang, and he excused himself and walked into a small room. He jotted some notes on a piece of paper, and headed back inside as he hung up the phone. His cell phone rang before he could get into the building.

"Hi Skip. What can I do for you? I'm very busy at the moment."

"I just called to say congratulations, Bro! Why didn't you ask me to be your best man?"

"Congratulations? Best man? What the Hay-Yil are you talking about, Skip?"

"Someone told me that you just got married. Who's the lucky girl? Diana?"

"Wrong. They got it wrong, Skip—I did not get married. A friend did. Who told you that I got married? Go back and tell them they're mistaken. I have to go toast the bride and groom. Good-bye." He quickly hung up.

A few minutes later, as the celebration was ending, Adam stood up and tapped a knife on the side of a water goblet to call everyone to pay attention. As the group conversation stopped, he said, "My friends, I have an announcement to make. I just got a phone call telling me that Juan and Esperanza have won an all-expense paid trip to Bermuda. Juan's and Esperanza's mouths dropped open and their eyes bulged out as they heard this announcement. "They fly out of DFW airport tonight at 8:40. They'll spend five days and four nights in the bridal suite of the Pompano Beach Club, a four-star hotel, before flying home to D/FW airport." The newlyweds screamed and squealed with excited approval.

Here Adam turned to the bride and groom and said, "We'll be happy to provide transportation to the airport for you two."

"*¡Si! Gracias. Acepto su amable ofrecimiento de alegría.*" Juan was too excited to notice he replied to Adam in Spanish. Adam understood the emotion behind the Spanish, and Diana translated it for him.

"In order to help the couple with expenses, Diana and I are each giving the couple a hundred dollar bill," here he paused and handed two C-notes to Juan, but Esperanza reached past Juan and grabbed the money and pushed it into her bosom before Juan could touch it. The wedding party roared their approval as Adam tried to continue talking, "And we invite all-a-y'all to give them a little spending money too." Immediately Juan's and Esperanza's families surrounded them, showering them with ten and twenty dollar bills and a few one- and five-dollar bills. And Juan kept repeating, "*Gracias, mi Padre Dios, Gracias.*"

Adam never even hinted that he was paying for the trip. In fact, the statement that he was giving the couple $100 prevented everyone present from imagining that Adam had anything to do with them winning a trip to Bermuda. But Diana knew—or she thought she knew.

Adam said, "Close your mouth, Diana, A bug may fly in."

"You did that, didn't you, Adam?"

"Did what?"

"You gave them a trip to Bermuda. When I tell you what Esperanza told me, you'll be doubly glad you did, too."

"It wasn't me."

With a teasing tone of voice she said, "You liar," and a moment later asking, "Who was it then?"

"Terry Realty in Plano," he said over the applause and cheers.

She laughed and said, "You duplicitous devil. So, you weren't lying— merely deceitfully misleading?"

"Right. I'm just a devil. Tell no one. What did Esperanza tell you?"

"First you have to promise to keep this a secret."

"Okay."

"Not good enough. Say it."

"I promise that I will keep secret whatever you tell me that you promised Esperanza you would never tell anyone."

"We were wrong, Adam. Sadly, Esperanza is not pregnant."

"Then why'd they get married weeks early?"

"Juan has cancer—terminal cancer."

"That is terrible. So that's why the family members were all crying at the wedding. Do the doctors say how long he has?"

"They say three to five weeks, maybe six. But you cannot let anyone know that you know."

"I won't. Unlike you, I know how to keep a secret. Maybe God will heal him."

"Yeah. That would really be good. Can God do that?"

He said, "I think so, and he thought, *The God of the Bible who rescued me from the plane crash wouldn't even break a sweat doing that.*

"She hopes he gets her pregnant before he dies."

Adam whispered, "Wow! Godspeed, *Hermano Juan y Hermana Esperanza Reyes*, Godspeed."

Without telling Adam, Diana made plans on the phone with Sherry Meadows to take Adam to Houston to see her and meet Gary, and their family. One Saturday Diana said, "Adam, let's go on a road trip tomorrow."

"Where do you want to go?"

"Humble." But she said it the way many locals do: 'Umble."

He mimicked her by asking, "Whut th' 'Ay-Yil's in 'Umble?"

"I have an uncle, aunt, and first cousins who live near there—and I haven't seen them in five or six years."

"Okay. I'll go—as long as I can also scout out Lake Houston."

"How long will that take?"

"Oh an hour or two maybe. We could ride the bikes down there." Diana had been talking about riding Caroline's Harley instead of selling it.

"No. we cannot interact much on the bikes."

"They both have two-way radios."

"That's not the same. We'll need to leave by six or six-thirty at the latest. It'll take us three and a half hours—if we have no problems. Check the Internet to see if there's any construction on Interstate 45."

"I could drop you off at your uncle's house and go to Lake Houston by myself."

"Why don't we play it by ear—we don't have to get back for anything. If we wanted to, we could even get a motel and come back on Sunday night or Monday morning."

"A motel? You're not, uh, trying to, uh, do something else here. Are you?"

She said, "No, I'm not. We can get separate rooms if you feel threatened."

He thought, *Separate motels might be sufficient.*

She said, "Maybe there's a church down there we could visit."

"Okay, you check into that and let me know what you find out."

Diana called Sherry to let her know Adam had agreed to take her to Houston, and that he was unaware of their scheme. She jotted down the name and address of the church Gary and Sherry attended, and what time the church service began so they'd know what time to leave. Sherry even told Diana where they would be sitting, and where she and Adam should sit.

Everything went like clockwork. Adam had no idea that Diana had a hidden purpose for this trip. The ride to Houston was uneventful. The weather was beautiful. The GPS directed them easily to Green's Bayou Church on the east side of Houston.

Adam saw Sherry, but he did not recognize her. Diana delayed their departure from the church. She told Adam she wanted to meet one or two of the church leaders. Then she had to find and use the restroom. After most parishioners had left, Gary and Sherry approached Diana and Adam. "Diana?"

"Yes."

"Welcome to Greens Bayou Church." Adam assumed this person was an old friend of Diana. *Small World*, he thought. Then Diana turned to him and said, "Adam, meet Gary and Sherry Meadows." This was a shock to Adam. He maintained his composure long enough to smile, shake Gary's hand, and say, "Nice to meet you"—but that greeting ended with him falling back on the cushioned pew with muffled bang. "Sheee" he began, but he did not finish that expletive in his usual way. Instead it came out as "She-Yoot."

Sherry smiled, "Adam, it's nice to see you again. You're looking well."

"Thank you." Adam was speechless. *Why didn't you warn me, Diana? I could have had a heart attack or something. If this shock doesn't kill me or restore my memory, nothing will.*

Gary said, "We'd like to take you to dinner somewhere. Is there anything in particular you like, Diana?"

"Almost anything except Italian food," but she was thinking of Adam.

Sherry agreed, "Adam never cared for Italian restaurants. I'd always have to go by myself."

Gary looked across the room and motioned for someone to join them. In a moment, four youngsters were standing between Gary and Sherry. She introduced them, "Kids, this is Adam Bowers. He was my first husband— I'm sure that you remember me talking about him." They smiled at each other, and Sherry continued, "Gary Junior finishes high school this year and has a scholarship to Texas A&M. We call him JR."

JR reached out to shake hands and say, "Pleased to meet you, sir."

"Ken is in the tenth grade." Ken repeated JR's polite handshake and greeting, except he said, "Nice to meet you, Mr. Bowers."

"Natalie is in the eighth grade, and Stephanie is in the fifth grade." The girls were shy and hardly made eye contact with Adam, but they repeatedly and furtively glanced up at Diana. In unison, the two girls said, "Nice to meet you."

"Wow! Beautiful girls and handsome boys—and so well mannered. I know you're proud of them."

"Thank you Diana. We thank God for blessing us with such good kids."

"So, JR is taking the children to eat some McFood and then home." As the children left, Gary said, "Will y'all join us for lunch?"

Adam and Diana looked at each other and agreed, "Sure. We'd like that."

Adam handed Diana the car keys, indicating he'd like her to drive, and they followed the Meadows. "So you planned all this behind my back? Why didn't you tell me?"

"Because that would have given you the chance to say, 'No'. And I did not want you to have that opportunity. Sherry and I talked about this over the phone. Are you mad at me?"

"No. I'm impressed with you, you duplicitous devil! Thanks for planning this. Sherry is still very attractive, but she could lose a few pounds and a few inches."

Diana said, "She's had four children, Adam!"

After they took their food choices to a table in a quiet corner of Luby's Cafeteria, they balanced eating with talking.

Diana said, "I've gone with Adam as he's visited a few churches in the north Dallas area, and this provokes me to ask you, Sherry, what do you and Gary like the most about Green's Bayou Church?"

"Gary and I have talked about this quite a bit. We like the fact that the children like the programs and activities that they have for them. The kids never say they don't want to go to church—they love it."

She looked at Gary for help, and he said, "We like the fact that the leadership of the church tries to teach and live out the message of the Bible. The pastor does not preach 'pop psychology' or 'postmodern philosophy.' His messages are biblical and relevant to our lives. He's not involved in the political fights of our era—a fact that some people do not like. The church also works at helping people grow in their faith in Christ."

"As a matter of fact, this is one of the most important things for me," Sherry said. "When we first arrived here, I thought I was a mature Christian. I soon discovered that I had much to learn. I also like the fact that Greens Bayou Church is doing the good works that demonstrate the love of Christ to people who live near us. We support orphanages, drug rehabilitation centers, safe houses for abused spouses, pregnancy counseling pointing people to alternatives to abortion, medical and dental care for the poor, and several other compassionate care ministries."

Gary continued, "A few years ago the entire church discussed this question: 'Can a Social Gospel and a Gospel of Salvation coexist in a Christian person or Christian church?' Some people thought it either cannot or should not. For the majority of those who stayed with the church, our answer was yes, we can and we should."

Sherry said, "Adam, can you tell us what motivated you to this God-Quest? What have you found so far? This news is pleasantly astonishing to me."

"If you'll allow me to postpone a full answer, I'd appreciate it. I'm under the care of psychiatrist, and in a few weeks I'll be giving him the long answer to your question. We're hoping that hard evidence will come to light establishing the fact that I was on that plane. I will send you the full report then."

"The short answer is this: Everyone on board that airplane perished when it crashed—except me. I had an experience in which an alien being or God rescued me from certain death—and he said it was for a purpose. Christianity is the only religion that I know of that is consistent with my experience, but there are so many forms of Christianity that I don't know which one—if any—to embrace.

"Let me ask you a question. What kind of Christians are y'all? And what denomination is Greens Bayou church?'

Gary spoke first, "The church is non-denominational. Many members were Methodists, Baptists, Presbyterian, Pentecostal, Nazarene—all Evangelical. Some members were agnostics, atheists, or nothing, and a growing number are former Catholics.

"While the church is not affiliated with a Pentecostal denomination, members who are Pentecostal have a freedom to exercise the gifts of the Spirit. Our pastor usually avoids preaching the doctrines that predictably segregate Christians into denominations. Over a year, he pretty much covers the essentials of the Christian faith."

"I thought your pastor's message this morning was good, Gary."

"What do you mean by 'good sermon'? Do you mean he challenged you to become more like Christ Jesus?"

"Uh…well, not directly."

"Do you mean he pointed out something God wants you to do, or to stop doing?"

"Ummm, not really."

"Do you mean how you felt when he finished preaching?"

"I felt good—but that's not what I meant. I did feel that God was pleased with me. Why do you ask?"

"When most people say, 'That was a good sermon,' they just mean that they agree with the points of that sermon or that it made them feel good. And when many people say, "That's a good 'translation of the Bible or that's a good 'Study Bible' or 'that's a good commentary,' they just mean that they like it—usually because it agrees with their position. Once a Christian friend told me, 'I want to read only those commentaries written by a scholar who's a part of my denomination. Then I know it's accurate.' I think he's mistaken to think his part of the Christian church has a franchise on God's Truth."

"You challenge me to think—in a good way. Gary, which translation of the Bible do you think I should read and study? What's the best translation?"

"Which translation of the Bible you read depends in part on why you are reading the Bible. If you are reading for personal edification, almost any modern English translation that you like will be more than adequate.

"If you want to argue with a seminary-trained minister, you might need a different Bible.

"If you use a study Bible, you should know that the notes at the bottom of the page do not have the authority of Scripture. They are similar to the ideas expressed in a commentary and should not be considered as part of God's Word.

"They can be very helpful, though. They offer the background of the author and the situation of the ancient target audience, and this can help us understand what the writer was saying.

"They often illuminate translation difficulties (like the range of meaning of Hebrew or Greek words in that time and place).

"And, they often clarify interpretation problems. Generally, a 'good' study Bible will present the variety of interpretations suggested through the years by scholarly believers, pointing out the strengths and weaknesses each of these interpretations. But they don't always tell the reader which interpretation is the 'right' one.

"I think God expects us to use the minds that he's given us. Faith in God is not an excuse for mindless ignorance or stupidity. Christians should respond to God's invitation to national Israel through the prophet Isaiah: "Come let us reason together" (1:18).

"So Christians should think analytically as we read a commentary, read notes in a study Bible, or hear someone teach or preach from the Bible. God does not suffer from multiple personality disorder, and the Bible says God cannot lie.

"At times, God's Word may be difficult for us to understand—but we should expect it to be understandable. God's not inscrutable. The big word is *perspicuity*. I believe in the perspicuity of the Bible—which simply means that is it understandable. Well, at least God's provision for our forgiveness and his design in the creation are easily understood by a person with average intelligence."

"How did you learn all this, Gary?" But he was thinking, *Gary sounds as committed and as knowledgeable as Juan. I'm glad Sherry is with him.*

"I grew up in a Christian home that read the Bible as a family. I've been studying the Bible for years—and we've had an awesome teacher in our pastor. I meditate on his messages all week. And our family reads and studies the Bible together from various English translations."

Chapter 14: Searching in Euless

Diana stopped brushing her hair long enough to answer the phone. She knew it was Adam. "Hello. Are you almost ready to go?"

"No. I don't feel well. I don't think I'll try to go to church this morning. They'll still be there next Sunday."

"I'm almost ready. Do you have a fever?"

"No. I just feel rotten. I'm going to try to sleep another hour or two. You can go without me."

"No. I don't want to do that. Do you want to plan to eat lunch later?"

"Probably. I'll call you when I get up."

"Okay. Bye."

Adam felt a little guilty because he did not go to church. He knew that he skipped out of laziness. Diana always went with him when he visited various Sunday morning church services. At first he thought she just wanted to be with him, but later he wondered if she had her own God-Quest.

One of Diana's friends at school had told her about a church she described as non-traditional in Euless, and Diana told Adam. They decided to visit that church this next Sunday, but they decided to meet the minister and learn a little about this church first. So one Monday, with the address in hand, Diana drove them west on highway 183 to Euless and found the church. The building was small. She parked the car, and they entered the sanctuary. An older man saw them, and, with a smile, said, "May I help you?"

"Oh, sorry. We just thought we'd look around. May we?"

"Sure. I didn't mean to startle you." He walked over to Adam, held out his hand and said, "I'm Rev. Rex Lord. I'm the minister of this church. Come in. I'll give you the grand tour, if you'd like. Or you could just sit and meditate or pray." Rev. Lord was an older man with white hair, bushy eyebrows, and a cherubic face and personality.

They shook hands and the conversation continued, "Father, my name is Adam. Adam Bowers and this is my friend, Diana Norris. We both live in Plano—but not together. One of Diana's friends told her about this church, we were in the neighborhood, and thought we'd see if anyone was here."

Diana spoke up, "It's nice to meet you, Rev Lord. I hope we've not caught you at a busy time. May we look around the church?"

"Diana, your distinctive voice and your black hair remind me of an actress from my boyhood days. I cannot recall her name."

"Was it Suzanne Pleshette?"

"Yes, it was. I'm amazed that you've heard of her—she was an actress before you were born. How did you guess her name?"

"Oh, through the years my father and my uncle have commented on the similarity. I hope you intended it as a compliment."

"It is a compliment. She was beautiful, had a lovely figure, and thick beautiful black hair. Her voice was sometimes referred to as husky or smoky, and I loved her low voice." Then Lord turned to Adam. "Tell me about yourself, Adam. What do you do? Where are you from? What line of work are you in? Are you a believer or a seeker or…something else?"

"I'm sorry, Father. I'm not able to answer your questions. I was in an accident recently and apparently I have a form of amnesia. I'm hoping something will trigger the restoration of my memory."

"Please, call me Rex. If you insist on using an honorific, Rev. Lord or Pastor Lord is more than sufficient—but I prefer Rex." By this time the two of them were seated on a pew near the front of the sanctuary.

"So, Rex, it's nice to meet you. I'd guess I've never been to church here, or you would recognize me."

"Right. Most of my parishioners are older than you—and even older than I am. But I don't recall ever seeing you before."

"Rex, d'you know God? I'd like to know God. Can you tell me how to know God?"

"Wow. That's a huge subject. I'll try to help. Some people summarize God in three words. Like, God is love—as if that is her only character trait. Others think only in terms of punishment and reward—Heaven and Hell. I prefer to think of God as an invisible force for good, rather than as a person. Adam thought, *God is female? Well, I guess that's no worse than thinking God is male.*

"Adam, we believe that enlightened humans are able to solve all of our problems. We no longer need the idea of a single all-powerful deity to help us. This church is dedicated to helping humans finding human solutions to human problems."

For just a second, Adam resonated with the idea that God is a force. *Whatever or whoever rescued me from that plane crash was extremely powerful—maybe All-Powerful.* But he quickly rejected Rex's concept of God as inconsistent with his recent personal experience—even though he could not articulate precisely what was wrong with Rex's descriptive image of God.

He courteously listened to Rex, but his interest quickly waned. As he left, Rex said, "Adam, I hope you'll come back. I lead a book study on Sunday morning. The discussion is quite animated. Many who attend have graduate degrees in theology or philosophy. Following the morning meeting, we all eat lunch together.

"We work to accomplish the Old Testament goal of social justice and try to carry on the earthly message of Jesus, that we love everyone, especially the marginalized and disenfranchised people in our society.

"In the afternoon, after lunch, we have a smaller group that discusses a book of the Bible. We are currently trying to establish which parts of the Gospel of Matthew are historical and which parts are fictitious. We're using the scholarly research of 'The Jesus Seminar.' Are you familiar with it?"

"No. I've never believed in God, but that could be changing. Rex, do you have a brochure describing this church? Maybe a website describing your core beliefs, your requirements for church membership, or something like that?"

"Goodness no. We don't embrace a creed. In order to become a member you just need to be a human and alive. Being willing to think and tolerant of those with an opinion different from your own is a big help too. We don't really care what you believe about God. We're more interested in what you believe about human beings. Come join the conversation any time, Adam."

"Thanks for the invitation, Rev. Lord." This left him feeling as if his confusion-level had just been increased by two orders of magnitude. *Why can't Christians agree on all important doctrines? If counterfeits exist, there must be a genuine, I guess. I have to remember to ask Juan about denominations.*

"Tell me. How can I know God the same way that you know God?"

"In order to know God, you must first have faith."

"You mean, I must have faith in God?"

"I just mean have faith; and it's easier to have faith in yourself and faith in other people than to have faith in an invisible, inscrutable God.

"Second, serve others as Jesus served others. Jesus taught, if you want to be first in God's kingdom, be servant of all. If you do this, then people can have faith in you.

"Third, work to overcome social injustice."

"What do you mean by 'social injustice'?"

"Human societies are full of poor people who are marginalized and disenfranchised because they are weaker. These people are usually dominated by the people in power. We have to work to overcome this domination by those in power. The disenfranchised includes widows and orphans, those forced to serve as sex slaves—the poor, who cannot afford food, clothing, lodging, medical care, and equal treatment under the law—the injustice may be based on race, gender, or ethnicity.

"Are you familiar with James Hunt's poem "Abou Ben Adhem"?

"I think we read it in junior high English class."

'Nothing sums up our central belief better than that. I memorized it as a child. Listen carefully to the words." And he closed his eyes, smiled, and recited it from memory.

"Abou Ben Adhem (may his tribe increase!)
    Awoke one night from a deep dream of peace,
"And saw—within the moonlight in his room,
    Making it rich and like a lily in bloom—
"An angel, writing in a book of gold.
    Exceeding peace had made Ben Adhem bold,
"And to the presence in the room he said,
    'What writest thou?'—The vision raised its head,
"And, with a look made of all sweet accord,
    Answered, 'The names of those who love the Lord.'
'And is mine one?' said Abou. 'Nay, not so,'
    Replied the angel. Abou spoke more low,
"But cheerly still, and said, 'I pray thee, then,
    Write me as one that loves his fellow men.'
"The angel wrote and vanished. The next night
    It came again with a great wakening light,
"And showed the names whom love of God had blessed,
    And lo! Ben Adhem's name led all the rest."

"It is a beautiful poem, and interesting. Couplets. How old is the poem?"

"I'm not sure—I think Hunt wrote it in the 1830s. I think that this summarizes the central message of Christianity, too. Why do you ask how old it is?"

"Idle curiosity. The poem equates loving people with loving God?"

"Yes. This is the central message of the Gospel of Christ: Love God by loving people. Both Mark and Luke record in their Gospels that Jesus said the same thing when he was asked to identify the greatest commandment:

"Love the Lord your God with all your heart and with all your soul and with all your mind and with all your strength.' The second is this: 'Love your neighbor as yourself.' There is no commandment greater than these."

Rev. Lord continued, "The only way we can express love to God is by loving people. The central message of the Gospels does not address the divinity of Jesus of Nazareth. It's about what Jesus taught and modeled in his life and death."

"I'm not sure I agree with you, but you've certainly given me something to think about. Thanks, Rex."

"In that case, I've been successful." They stood up and Rex said, "Well, I hope you'll come back and be with us again. You'll find us to be reflective and quite thought provoking at times."

They shook hands and Adam said, "Thanks."

As Adam and Diana left church to find a nearby Thai restaurant, he said, "This was my favorite ethnic food?"

"Very favorite." After they were seated and looking at a menu, Diana said, "I don't think you ever ate any Thai food that you didn't like. But your favorites were red curry, green curry, panang, thom kha gai, and mee krob. Different Thai restaurants spell some of these dishes differently on their menus."

""How often did I eat in Thai restaurants?"

"Oh, one to five times a week—sometimes twice in one day, lunch."

"So do you think this might prime and restart my memory pump?"

"Possibly. It could. It should."

The Asian waitress asked, "May I take your order, sir?" When Diana answered the waitress, the waitress turned to face her.

Diana said, "Yes, thank you. An appetizer of thom ka gai for each of us, And we will share these entrées: pad thai, green curry with chicken, mee krob, and shrimp prik king. Please make the last three dishes moderately spicy. He would like beer, any Thai brand, and I will have Thai iced coffee."

"Very good, ma'am."

After their food and drinks arrived, she asked him, "Adam, where do you see our relationship going?"

"I'm not sure what you're asking me. Keep eating and be blunt."

"Do you think we'll ever have a sexual relationship? Do you think we'll ever marry? Have kids? Have a life together?" She glanced at him to gain anything his body language might reveal during his answer. Adam seemed to choke on this food.

"I don't know. But we'll never have sex unless we're married."

"Is that a proposal?"

"No. But I hope it's a fact."

"Is your opinion controlled by memories of Caroline?"

"I'm not sure. I'm not even sure why I feel so strongly about it. At first I thought it was out of loyalty to Caroline. But I wonder now if it's related to my God-Quest."

"Do you think God will be more inclined to bless your quest if you're celibate?"

"I don't think so—Maybe—I don't know."

"Do you like the dishes we ordered?'

"They're all great. I see why Thai food is my favorite."

"I've never eaten thom ka gai before. Thanks for introducing it to me. What would you order if you ate in another Thai restaurant?"

"Either green curry again or a dish I don't recall eating before. With my amnesia, that's most of them."

"Did anything bring back a memory?"

"Not that I noticed. But I've not tasted the mee krob yet. So please hand it to me, and I'll see if it helps." It didn't.

They had their waitress put what they could not eat in disposable Styrofoam containers to take home with them.

The next Tuesday evening at dinner, as Adam and Diana were sitting with Juan and Esperanza discussing their meeting with Rex Lord, Adam said, "Maybe Rex Lord is right. Maybe we should understand Jesus as a great teacher and example of ethical life. Would that be justifiable, Juan?"

"Some people argue that position, Adam. But C. S. Lewis—in a book titled *Mere Christianity*—had what I think is the best response to that position. Have you ever heard of C.S. Lewis?

"No, I've never heard of him."

"In that case, let me say his name again a little louder." Juan almost shouted when he said, "C.S. Lewis!" Then he continued in a conversational volume. "I'm sure that you've heard of him now. Lewis was a professor of English Literature at Cambridge University in England. Just a second, I might be able to find it online." Juan accessed the Internet with his iPhone and found the quote in a few minutes. He announced, "Found it, page 40. Let me read it to you.

"I am trying here to prevent anyone saying the really foolish thing that people often say about him: "I'm ready to accept Jesus as a great moral teacher, but I don't accept his claim to be God."

Thinking Juan had finished quoting Lewis, Adam interrupted him, "That's almost exactly what Rex said—except the 'prevent' part, of course."

Mildly annoyed by the interruption, Juan said, "Do you want me to read the rest of it?"

"There's more? Sure, read it."

"I'll start over at the beginning." This time Juan emphasized the first sentence by reading it more slowly and a little louder.

"I am trying here to prevent anyone saying the really foolish thing that people often say about him: "I'm ready to accept Jesus as a great moral teacher, but I don't accept his claim to be God." That is the one thing we must not say. A man who was merely a man and said the sort of things Jesus said would not be a great moral teacher. He would either be a lunatic—on a level with the man who says he is a poached egg—or else he would be the Devil of Hell. You must take your choice. Either this man was, and is, the Son of God; or else a madman or something worse. You can shut him up for a fool, you can spit at him and kill him as a demon; or you can fall at His feet and call him Lord and God. But let us not come with any patronizing nonsense about his being a great human teacher. He has not left that open to us. He did not intend to."

This time Adam waited a few seconds to be certain that Juan had finished, and then said, "Wow. Email that to me, please. What choices: a poached-egg lunatic, a Devil of Hell, or the Son of God. Did Lewis ever write anything else?"

"Several things. But the book I think you'd enjoy the most is how God changed him from being an atheist into a believer."

"He was an atheist? Tell me the name of that book, please?"

"*Surprised by Joy: The Shape of My Early Life*."

"Is it still in print?

"I saw it on Amazon not too long ago, or you could probably find it cheaper in a used bookstore. Why?"

"Maybe I'll stop and buy it on our way home."

"Adam, are you familiar with the English philosopher Anthony Flew?"

"Yes, but only because my friend Skip mentioned him to me recently. He was a famous atheist philosopher who became a theist several years ago."

"Right. Do you know what changed his mind about God's existence?"

"No. Skip just said that Flew's change of mind had no effect on our atheistic position years ago."

"In a nutshell, Flew finally thought the scientific support for a universe that seemed designed for life, including human life, was now so strong, that he had to admit the evidence for a Designer was greater than the evidence against it."

"And you tell me this because…?"

"I think you should read and think about this too."

"Where do I easily find material to read on this?

"Probably the easiest to access is material written published by The Discovery Institute in Seattle and often written by philosopher Stephen Meyer—who is also a Christian. Read *Darwin's Doubt*."

"Juan, what's the 'Jesus Seminar'?"

"Where did you hear about the Jesus Seminar, Adam?"

"Rev. Lord said they're using it to study the New Testament Gospels."

Juan said, "Back in the mid-1980s a group of liberal Bible scholars decided they would pool their efforts and redact the four Gospels in the New Testament. The goal of the Seminar was to review each of the sayings and deeds attributed to Jesus in the four Gospels and determine which of them could be considered authentic. They decided to publicize their findings to the general public, rather than just to a handful of scholars who specialize in studying the Gospels. They published their work in a book entitled, *The Five Gospels: The Search for the Authentic Words of Jesus*, but it's more like a search of events and words of Jesus that they can dismiss as fictional.

Robert Funk, Roy Hoover, and the Jesus Seminar were listed as the authors. They used five different font colors to identify the most likely to the least likely sayings and deeds of Jesus of Nazareth.

"I don't know of anyone who takes their work seriously—except maybe a few other liberal scholars. Wilkins and Moreland wrote a book that demonstrated the fallacies in the work in *Jesus under Fire: Modern Scholarship Reinvents the Historical Jesus.*

"Adam, you'll learn that not every group that claims the label *Christian* is really Christian."

"So I'm discovering, Juan, how do you know so much about the Bible and Christianity?"

"I've been working at it for years. It's a labor of love for Christ, and it has been my passion for over ten years.

"I want to be faithful."

Chapter 15: Weekend Bike Trip

"Adam, this is Frank Noble. Listen, we're riding bikes down to Austin, then to Port Aransas in a couple of weeks. We'll have anywhere from twenty to thirty bikes in a convoy. Would you like to ride with us?"

H said Port Aransas as many native Texans do, as one word: *Porteransas.*

"Sure, but I'll have to give you an answer later. I have to make sure I'm not already scheduled to do something else. Where is Port Aransas? When do you plan to return?"

"It's on Mustang Island, just past Corpus Christi, and we plan to drive back on Saturday—400 miles, and some change. All it'll cost you is your gas and food—we plan to camp out on the beach. Oh, we'll get motel rooms in Austin one night on our way back.

"The bike pack will be followed by a van in case of break-downs. This will give you a chance to meet several of our church members."

"Are the ladies invited?"

"Not on this trip. We do on several shorter trips. But most of the ladies don't care for camping on the beach. Apologize to Diana for me. Does she like to camp?"

"Yes. Not a problem. And I have an extra belt on board—just in case."

"Great. Send me a text or an email if you have other questions."

"Will do. Thanks, Frank."

"You bet. I hope you make it."

"Me too."

Later, when he told Diana about the trip, she replied, "Perfect timing. I have a big exam to prepare for, so—ride carefully. And don't forget your cell phone and charger."

"I'm looking forward to getting to know some of the men from BCC."

The weather was perfect when the bikers lined up in the church parking lot. The men drank coffee while they waited for the sun to get a little higher in the sky. Pastor No-Bull was the only rider that Adam already knew. After introduction to the other riders, Adam could not recall any names—they were all just a jumble in his mind.

"Adam, you're the newbie this trip. Would you rather ride up front, in the middle, or at the back?"

"At the back, thanks, Rev. Noble." The group laughed when Adam called him Rev. Noble.

As the laughter died down, Noble said, "Just call me Frank, Mr. Bowers. Pretend we're friends." This comment prolonged the laughter. Frank turned to a young man with long hair and introduced him to Adam.

"Adam, this is Jack Blake—a.k.a. 'Black Jake' or 'Hi-Jack'. You and he will be partners on this trip. Is that okay?"

"Sure. Hi, Jack. Good to meet you."

"You too, Adam. If you have any questions, just ask me."

"Thanks. I will."

A tall man wearing a brown leather jacket with a logo of some kind on the back took charge of the group. "We'll be using channel 7 on this trip, so set your radios to channel 7. I hope you all filled your tanks with gas, because we don't plan to stop for fuel until we get near Austin. If you have a problem with this, come tell me now." He paused, but no one was forthcoming.

While he was waiting, Adam walked to one side to see what was on the back of his jacket. Finally he could see it clearly enough to read: "Christian Motorcyclists Association." Later on the trip he noticed about half of the men had a shirt or another jacket, or hat with the same logo.

"Please remember that people will recognize us a group of Christian bikers. So let's honor Christ in all we say and do. I know that some of you enjoy a beer or a glass of wine, and some of you are teetotalers. We respectfully ask that you not drink alcohol while on this trip. Thank you. Pastor Frank, if you will ask God to protect us, we'll head south."

"Thanks, Bud. Men, please pray with me. Father, may our actions be consistent with our confession of faith in you. Please protect us as we travel. Thank you for sending Jesus to redeem us."

Adam was startled as all the men simultaneously said, "Amen." He did not realize that Frank's last sentence thanking God for the Redeemer was the signal for them to say "Amen." Before the trip was over, Adam was able to join that chorus of amens.

The procession was two bikes wide and twelve bikes long, and Jack and Adam were at the very end. The convoy was followed by a van with a trailer a safe distance behind them. About half of the bikes were Harleys, and the rest were Honda Gold Wings, a Triumph, and an Indian. All of the bikes had saddlebags or a T-bag, except the one with a trailer.

Every time the group stopped, Jack would tell Adam something. Once, he said, "The guy in front of you is named Jerry, and he's the CEO of a local television station, channel 5. He moved to Texas from Chicago—by himself. His wife refused to move, and divorced him. He's in a major life crisis."

Another time, Jack said, "The biker in front of me is Phil; he works as a chemist for Texaco. He has been a Christian for less than a year. He recently moved to Duncanville, but drives his family to Plano for church every Sunday morning. He almost never misses."

The trip to Austin was completed without problems. Some men shared a motel room—two or three or four to a room—to save money. Jack and Adam shared a room, but Adam paid for it. The ride to Port Aransas was scenic and without incident or accident. Adam was getting to know and like Black Jake who was several years younger than he.

When they arrived at Stewart Beach next to Nueces County Park near Port Aransas, a half a dozen men went to the van and unpacked and set up the tents, while another half-dozen searched for firewood, but Adam was unsure what to do. So he said, "Jack, what's our job? Should we help someway?"

"No. You're our guest, and I'm your guide. We're doing what we're supposed to do. Just watch."

"I've never eaten food this good when camping, Frank! How do they do it?"

"I'm glad you like it. We have three men who take care of the whole meal. For them, it's a labor of love. On our way home on Saturday, we'll eat at a restaurant between Georgetown and Temple. The food's pretty good there too."

"Are these road trips really just an excuse to eat?" Frank laughed with Adam.

After everyone had finished eating, a few men began policing the area, picking up paper plates, plastic glasses, and trash—most of it their own. Within a few minutes, most of men were seated around picnic tables or in camp chairs. Then someone put a match to the collected firewood, producing a medium-sized bonfire in just a few minutes.

Frank stood up and said, "Adam, come up here and stand with me please." Adam was caught completely off-guard. He took a minute or two, and reluctantly he sauntered to where Frank was standing.

"Guys, I'm sure you have all heard about the plane crash near Waco a few months ago. You know that everyone on board perished. Everyone, that is, except Adam Bowers. Adam, would you take a few minutes and tell this group what you experienced on that flight?"

Adam was flustered. He did not like speaking in public to a group any larger than one person. *Why didn't Frank prepare me for this?* he wondered. *What would he do if I just said 'no thanks, I don't want to speak in public'?*

So he looked Frank in the eyes and quietly said, "I'm really not much of a public speaker. This is awkward. I'm not really a Christian."

Frank did not flinch. He replied, "Just relax and tell them men what you experienced. Tell them that you're not a Christian. Adam they will love you anyway—trust God's Holy Spirit to help you."

With that Frank walked away, and the group applauded Adam.

"Men. Frank." He nodded at the group and the pastor as be said these two words. "I will not pretend that I'm something other than what I am. Two things I'm not: I am neither a Christian nor a public speaker. One of these may be changing, but I know you'll be disappointed in what I say tonight. If I say anything offensive, please forgive me, I apologize in advance."

He took a deep breath, cleared his throat, muttered under his breath, and said, "A few months ago, I was on top of the world. My business was doing very well."

But someone shouted, "What the name of your business?" so loudly that Adam was startled and forgot what he'd already said.

"Realty. Terry Realty. In Plano."

Several of the group looked at each other and said nice things about Terry Realty and Plano.

Adam thought, *Are these clowns going to interrupt me every sentence?* He paused so long, that one of the guys prompted him, "Keep going, Adam, tell us more." And the group chuckled at that wisecrack.

Adam gained a little more confidence. "I will continue, but you clowns need to cut me some slack. I'm no Day-Yim good at public speaking. So please save your questions and comments until my birthday. Write them on a card, put a C-note in the card, and mail it to me. Now where was I?" Adam had no idea that this group thought his use of a vulgar expletive was inappropriate.

"I was on top of the world. Healthy. Prosperous. Enjoying life and friends. I had been very active as an atheist for about twelve years. First as a student at the University of Texas," he paused for the UT fans in the group to give a boisterous UT shout-out, "Longhorns" and "Bevo!" then continued, "and then later in the Dallas area. I've been told that some of my friends called me 'The Apostle of Atheism'—behind my back.

"To some people, I claimed to be an agnostic—but that was only because I did not want my atheism to hurt my business. We live in 'The Bible Belt,'—some say 'The Buckle of the Bible Belt.'

"To Christian people, I would claim that I was open to God revealing himself to me—but that was not true. I was angry with God over the death of my parents and the death of a baby boy my wife and I had. We've been divorced for years.

"Caroline, my fiancée—soon to be my second wife, or so I thought—and I boarded a plane to go to Cancún for a four-day romantic getaway. The plane crashed south of Waco—as Frank just told you—and I was the lone survivor. I lost my luggage, my fiancée, and my memory. And I could possibly lose my atheism."

The group of men became very reverent and silent as Adam continued, "How is it possible that I survived? God rescued me. It doesn't make any sense. Why would God rescue me, and allow Caroline—a wonderful nurse who finished parochial school near the top of her class and nursing school as the top student—to perish? I thought that God had made a mistake! The police are not satisfied yet that I was really on that plane, even though all evidence suggests that I was—except the fact of my survival.

"I'll tell you only one other thing about this divine rescue. When God saved me from the plane, he said to me, 'You claim you don't know if I exist. Well, now you know Adam, I am.'

"My doctor diagnosed me with retrograde amnesia, probably caused by multiple traumas. I have regained very little of my memory, and may never regain all of it. I am still trying to find out who I am.

"When he rescued me, God told me that it was for a purpose. But I've not discovered what that purpose is yet.

"Thanks for listening to me."

Frank was at Adam's side and said, "Adam, before you sit down, would it be okay if we pray with you—for you?"

"I guess so. What are you going to ask God to do?" He sounded a little apprehensive.

"Just to restore your memory and bring you to faith in Christ."

"Yeah, those are both good."

He had no idea that every man there wanted to pray with him, so when the group stood and walked as one person toward him, he was startled again and flinched. Frank held him steady as men reached out to touch him by placing a hand on his shoulder or back or head. The cacophony of two dozen men praying aloud at the same time was intimidating to Adam, but he felt no fear, just intense, compassionate, sincere support.

Later he told Diana, "The feeling was like the feeling of coming home. I belong here."

The ride back home on Saturday was not uneventful. The sky was partly cloudy. The temperature was in the high 60s with no forecast of rain. On the way back, the group did not stay in a motel in Austin, but rode the 400-plus miles home with only two stops planned for fuel and bathroom. The group had two stops planned—barring a breakdown or an accident.

As they approached Dallas at 70 miles per hour on Interstate 35E, somewhere between Loop 12 and the highway 67 interchange, a careless driver drifted over into the right lane. Jack was on Adam's left, and the inside lane was on Jack's left. At first, Jack did not see the car drift over into the right lane. By the time he saw the danger, it was too late. Jack over-reacted. He swerved and almost hit Adam's bike. Everything happened so fast that no two accounts of the accident to the police were identical. Fortunately, no vehicle was close behind Jack and Adam, or it would have been even more disastrous.

Jack's bike fell, and he and the bike went their separate ways. Adam maintained control of his bike—just barely, but he made a panic stop. The driver of the car that caused the accident sped up and drove on. All but two of the BCC bikers stopped—two of the men accelerated, caught up with the car fleeing the accident, and wrote down the tag number.

Adam put the kickstand down, shut the engine off, and ran back to Jack, who was unconscious and lying in the middle of the right hand lane. He debated with whether or not he should move Jack so that no one could run over him.

In a few minutes that seemed like a few hours, an ambulance and EMTs were on the scene helping Jack. By now the BCC team was all standing around Jack trying to discover how injured he was. At first they thought he was dead, because he was unconscious and unresponsive. But the EMTs worked furiously to immobilize him and get him in the ambulance and on his way to the hospital. The BCC group followed the ambulance to Presbyterian Hospital, about 15 miles away.

They made several phone calls. Frank traveled home to get his car and Susan, Jack's wife to take her to the hospital. Several of the BCC men were still there about an hour and a half later when Frank returned. But the news was not optimistic.

One of the men told them, "He is alive, but we don't know how bad he's injured. They said that one leg and one of the bones in his left forearm are broken. They rushed him to surgery. They told us the reason, but we don't remember the words."

The men gathered around Frank, who asked, "Have you prayed together as a group yet?"

Several men answered, "No. Only individually."

"In that case, let's pray with Susan now. She's close to hysterical with anxiety. Just lead us in prayer as you feel God leading you."

An older man said, "Father, please deliver Jack like you saved Adam."

Another said, "Dear God, please preserve my friend today."

A third said, "Demonstrate your mercy, grace, and love in Jack, Father."

Then Frank summed up their prayers, "God we ask in ignorance, not knowing what your purpose is. But if this can be your will for Jack and Susan, whether you use modern medicine or ancient miracle, please restore

Jack to his family and to our part of the Body of Christ. Thank you for Father for sending Jesus to die for us." And all of them said "Amen."

As they were talking and grieving together, the doctors approached and asked, "Are any of you related to the victim?"

Susan spoke up, "I'm Jack's wife."

"We're pretty sure he suffered no head trauma. His spleen was damaged in the accident and was hemorrhaging. He lost a lot of blood. Fortunately for him, the EMTs got him to the ER quickly. We had no choice but to remove his spleen to stop the bleeding. He has two broken bones: his left ulna and left fibula." The doctor pointed to his forearm and his calf to indicate the location of the breaks. "He has some contusions, severe abrasions, and other minor injuries, and he'll probably take a month or more to go back to work, but we expect him to recover—unless he has an injury that we overlooked. We want to keep him for observation at least overnight, and maybe a day or two more."

Susan said, "Thank you, doctor." Then she closed her eyes and said, "Thank you, God."

Several people exclaimed, "Praise God!" Susan bowed her head and wept bitterly. Adam realized that his fear of dying had been intensifying the past few months. He wondered, *Does this growing fear have any connection to my God-quest?* At times the thought, *It's just a matter of time before God comes for me.* He told no one about it—not Diana, not Dr. Bailey, and not Juan.

Oveer the next month, Jack had a least two friends join his wife in visiting Jack at the hospital. The men took an offering, and gave Susan five-hundred dollars to use any way she needed to.

Frank and his wife visited Susan at home and convinced Susan to allow the church to pay their mortgage and car notes for at least one month. Every day for two weeks, someone would bring cooked food to Jack and Susan's home for a meal for her and their children. Adam and Diana were pleased to learn to be allowed to do this once.

Adam silently prayed asking God to supernaturally calm his fear, as he had done when he rescued Adam from the plane.

Chapter 16: Second Faith Crisis

When Adam arrived at Panera, Juan was on his cell phone. Adam didn't mean to eavesdrop, but he could not help but hear that Juan was talking to customer service at some business—and he was very angry. He assumed that Juan was listening to the customer service representative during his long pauses.

He firmly but calmly said, "No, ma'am. That is not satisfactory." He paused, listening to the lady on the other side of that conversation.

"Well your company's motto is 'satisfaction guaranteed or your money back,' and I assure you, ma'am, I am not satisfied." He paused, listening again.

Over the next few moments, Juan said, "No ma'am" four times. "Ma'am, I don't think you can tell how angry I am since I am not using any vulgar language. However, I was in the military for four years, so let me tell you if you need me to use profane language in order to convince you that I am extremely angry and will pursue this until I get satisfaction, just tell me and I can recite some of those words for you."

Apparently the customer service representative did not need to hear those words, because Juan did not use them. Adam's mind wandered until Juan finished talking on the phone.

As soon as he hung up the phone, Juan said, "That woman drives me crazy! I explained the problem to her three times, and she still did not understand it. Give me a minute, Adam, for my anger to evaporate."

A moment later, Adam said "Okay. Tell me, Juan, why do you never use profanity? Is it because you're a Christian and this is part of Christianity?"

"I have a few reasons, and I'll tell them to you in no particular order—except the first one is really the only one that matters. I try not to use those vulgar words because they dishonor my Savior and Master, Jesus Christ. I do not want to say or do anything that would dishonor Christ.

"Also, years ago I formed the opinion that many people who habitually use profanity had a limited vocabulary, and I wanted to sound educated. I've found that I don't need these so-called 'power words' to argue forcefully."

"Power words? Why do you call them that?"

"Because people think by using this language, they're demonstrating to the hearer that they can argue more powerfully. Another common label is to call them 'taboo words.' As a Christian, God's Spirit is my power."

"Why have you never told me that I should stop using vulgar language?"

"I don't need to. One day God's Spirit will convict you—and you'll be obedient to him. But I hope you will never be like one lady in my church who is proud she uses no vulgar language, but she gossips constantly."

"Does the New Testament say anything about profane language?"

"The book of James talks about 'the tongue—and Paul's letter to Timothy and to the church at Ephesus also comments on what believers say. Both Matthew and Luke record Jesus as saying something like, 'out of the overflow of the heart, the mouth speaks'."

"I thought Christians just did not use these words to impress others with their 'holier-than-thou' character. What makes a word a taboo word? Isn't it just cultural?"

"It does have a cultural component, but I think it's more than culture. And it should be—for Christians."

"Juan, what about Hell? Do you think Hell is real? Or just a metaphor?"

"Some people just define Hell as eternal separation from God. Years ago, when I was a rookie believer, I asked a priest this same question about the reality of Hell. His reply to me was 'Juan, if you're going to believe what the Bible teaches about God and Heaven, you probably should also believe what it teaches us about the Devil and Hell.' That works for me. God does not require me to understand everything, but he does require me to believe in him."

"There's something else I've wanted to discuss with you for a long time."

"What is it?"

"I've been reading 1 Corinthians. St. Paul scolds the church there for their division into small competing splinter groups. Would God or Paul rebuke Christians today for denominations? Are denominations a contemporary parallel to the divisions in the church in Corinth that Paul condemned?"

"That's possible, and there are other possibilities that seem to be more likely, considering the context in 1 Corinthians. In addition to all the biblical prescriptions and proscriptions regarding appropriate worship, God seems to have left some room for personal tastes. And these personal preferences are probably shaped by our culture or subculture and our personality. An introverted person might be more relaxed and open to God's Spirit in a liturgical church. An extroverted person might be more relaxed and open to God's Spirit in a less liturgical church. Not everyone is comfortable hugging or holding hands with a stranger—especially during flu season."

"I guess it's possible that denominations are less evidence of the fragmentation of the Body of Christ, and more evidence of the diversity of the Body of Christ."

"So why are you loyal to the Catholic Church? Do you sincerely believe every teaching of the Catholic Church?"

"I privately admit that I have unanswered questions regarding transubstantiation of the bread and wine in the Eucharist. Are we cannibals? Does God miraculously change the bread into Jesus' human flesh and miraculously change the wine into Jesus' human blood? It's certainly possible, but I have doubts because it still tastes like wine to me. And I don't pray to Mary or any of the deceased saints But I also have criticisms of the way my Christian brothers at Protestant churches practice Communion and baptism.

"I especially find it odd that one Protestant group that argues we must baptize in water the same way that the early church baptized in water, or it is not baptism at all—freely changes the biblical unleavened bread and wine to leavened bread and grape juice. Would you use popcorn and apple juice for Communion if unleavened bread and wine were available? I doubt it. If we Christians are free to modify The Lord's Supper to fit our contemporary tastes, why are we not free to modify water baptism?

'So tell me why you don't drink alcoholic beverages. Does the Bible instruct Christians not to drink?"

"Some Christians claim the wine that Jesus drank or the wine that he miraculously produced at the wedding feast in Cana was nonalcoholic. Some groups consider drinking beer or wine as wrong—even though the Bible does not forbid it. The New Testament instructs Christians not to get drunk. But this raises the question of how they could get drunk on non-alcoholic wine—perhaps another miracle. In 1 Corinthians, Paul warned Christians not to do things that can enslave people—and alcohol fits that description. As my mother told me, 'Juan, if you never drink, you'll never be in danger of becoming drunk or an alcoholic.

"Wisdom would probably lead most people to enjoy life without alcoholic beverages.

"This would be a useful exercise for you, Adam. You may wait for a two or three years before doing this. Divide a piece of paper into four columns with lines. Write headings at the top of each column: 'Absolutely Essential' to the Christian faith, which are 'Important,' which are 'Probably True,' and which are 'Peripheral'—even if they are true. Then list under each heading a church doctrine or practice. Christians tend to lump all the teachings of their church in the first category or the first two categories."

"I probably don't know enough about Christianity to do that yet."

"You're probably right. Learn more first."

"Juan, how did you learn so much about the Bible and Christianity? You said that you worked hard. How?"

"I was in my last year of high school when I came to faith in Christ. I've always loved to read and study, so it was just natural for me to learn everything I could about my faith. I've read many books—including the Bible. For a while, I contemplated studying for the priesthood.

"At first, most of the books I studied had the imprimatur of the Catholic Church. Then I wanted to learn all I could from non-Catholics, so I've audited one course at several seminaries in the Dallas-Fort Worth area: Dallas Theological Seminary, Southwestern Baptist Theological Seminary, Perkins Seminary at SMU, and another online."

"What do you mean, you audited one course?"

"I always sat in a class over the same subject, 'hermeneutics.' I didn't want the credits, I just wanted the knowledge. Hermeneutics is the art and science of interpretation. I wondered if the different Christian groups had different methods of interpreting the Bible."

"And? What did you find?"

"Not too much difference. Catholics tend to put more emphasis on how the Church has historically understood a part of the Bible. Some Protestants interpret everything through God's covenants through human history, other Protestants interpret the Bible through something called 'dispensationalism'—which you'll encounter one day, but not now—and still others interpret God's Word in light of *heilsgeschichte*, a German word that means they interpret in light of the history of God's salvation through grace. Still others these think the best principle to include is the interpretation of the Bible in light of the rest of the Bible canon."

"Which model is the best?"

"I'm not sure. Maybe each of them has its usefulness and no one model is best. I'm not positive"

"Do you plan to study Hebrew and Greek one day, too?"

"No. I'm familiar enough with the languages to use some of the tools, but in order to critique a translation of Scripture, a person needs to master the biblical language, not just become familiar enough with it to stumble around. I know enough to read and understand the scholars, but I'm limited to comparing English language translations."

"Juan, you are my most trusted Christian friend. Well, my only Christian friend, I guess, except Esperanza."

"I'll tell you the same thing that Paul wrote in the 11th chapter of First Corinthians: 'Imitate me, then, just as I imitate Christ'. And I will add, in whatever way I fail to follow Christ, don't imitate me, Adam."

Diana was excited as she told Adam about the two concert tickets she got that afternoon, and she begged him to take her to hear Alison Krauss and Union Station in concert in Austin. She said, "I saw them a few years ago, and I'd heard that they're coming back to Texas. A lawyer friend at work got two passes to The Moody Theater, where Austin City Limits is recorded. He cannot go, so he gave the tickets to me. Please take me, Adam. I really want to go! Please? Please?"

Adam had only heard Krauss twice, once on TV's "Austin City Limits" and another time in the movie *O Brother Where Art Thou?* Adam especially liked the sound of her rendition of "There Is a Reason" on *ACL*—but he did not understand the meaning of the lyrics. To be fair, he didn't understand every word of the lyrics. Adam was definitely interested in going to this concert for merely the cost of traveling to Austin and back.

"I'd really like to go too, Diana. And we will go, but I want to talk to you about something else right now. Please listen to me without getting angry. Don't get on the defensive."

"I won't. I mean, I'll try not to. Why so serious? What is it?"

"You're a very attractive person. You have an exquisite face, a great figure, beautiful skin and hair, and when you smile, you light up a football stadium. You also have very cute ears,"

Diana smiled to hear this praise. "Awww…you sweet-talking flatterer. You'll have to do worse than that for me to get angry."

"That was not flattery. But…"

"Okay, here comes the 'Big Butt' part."

He ignored her playful comment, and said, "Diana, I don't like it when you use your feminine charms to manipulate people to do your will. That's petty, not pretty. Please don't do that to me. Ask me, and if the answer is no, accept it. Don't pout, now."

"I'm trying not to pout. No one enjoys being rebuked. I guess I'm not aware that I manipulate people." She looked at him and said, "Do I do that often?"

"Only when you don't get your own way." They were silent for a few seconds.

With a serious tone of voice, she said, "I guess I don't realize that I'm doing that. How do I learn to recognize and change it?"

"I don't know. I doubt you'd like it if I pointed it out to you ever time you do it again."

She broke eye-contact and said, "I'm sure you're right."

"Now that I've told you about it…?"

She looked him in the eyes, "I'll work to notice and change it. I agree that it is not an attractive trait in anyone. Be patient. I probably learned to do that begging daddy when I was a little girl twenty-something years ago, and it may be difficult to change in a week."

"Okay. Let me go get ready. Where d'you want to eat—in Dallas or in Austin?"

"Austin, at Thai House."

"Of course. Me too."

Diana said, "Don't forget to shave."

"I shaved this morning."

"I know. But your beard's so dark and heavy that you need to shave again by afternoon."

"In that case, I'll shave, shower, and get changed in the front bathroom—the shower in Caroline's bathroom is too small."

As he was locking the door, finding a towel, adjusting the water temperature, and stripping off his clothing, he noticed a brassiere hanging near the shower. For two or three minutes he just stood there staring at the bra. He thought it was Caroline's, and as Adam stared at it, he visualized Caroline. He remembered hugging and kissing her and the aroma of another of the perfumes she liked to wear. He remembered their passionate love making, and—for the first time in his life—he had a sense of personal sinfulness and himself as deserving God's punishment. He thought, *I must ask Juan to define sin—Is this even listed in the Ten Commandments? I don't think so. I recall only two of the Ten Commandments—one about lying and one about stealing. I'd better review that in the Bible.*

He thought of these things as he quickly showered and dressed. He tried to control his excitement over his anticipation of telling Diana that he had remembered more—much more—about Caroline. Fortunately, before he finished his shower, he realized, *Telling Diana is not a good idea.*

Diana drove the SUV to Austin that evening. They ate Thai food near the university, and arrived at The Moody Theatre in time to get in line. It wasn't long before volunteers confirmed their passes and put a wristband on them.

"Before we find our seats, Diana, let's use the restrooms." She waited in the hall for him, and, when he walked out, she smelled smoke on him.

"Do you recognize that smoke, Adam? Can you identify it"

"The aroma of that smoke is familiar—but I cannot place it. Don't tell me what it is. Let me try to remember it. I've been asking myself where I've smelled that aroma before."

"If I had to guess, Adam, I'd say you probably smelled it when you were in school here in Austin. Did you ever go to a rock concert?"

"Yes, but I don't recall who I heard. But I know that smoke. It's not cigar smoke. It's pipe smoke."

"Pipe smoke?" she echoed with rising inflection and raised eyebrows and a smile that said, "I don't think so."

"Yes, smoke from a pot-filled bong." His voice had a measure of pride. "I'm remembering some things. So far today I've recalled another memory of Caroline, and just now I recalled the aroma of weed burning," Adam cheerfully gave thanks. "I'm starting to regain my memory!" His joy produced this trifecta: "She-Yit! Why the Hay-Yil can't I quit using those Day-Yim vulgar words?" He thought, *It's a habit. God help me to lose this bad habit.*

At intermission, he remembered and told Diana, "Chicago. Deep Purple. Rod Stewart. Nitty Gritty Dirt Band. The Who."

Diana waited a moment before she said, "There's no way you heard all of those groups at one concert. Maybe over four years, when you were a student at UT. Did you smoke weed and go to rock concerts as a student?"

"I guess you're right, but I don't remember. I'm not completely positive I even saw all those groups. Maybe I just recall the names of those groups."

"Diana, you seem to be very interested in my God-Quest."

"Yes, I am. But we may have different approaches and goals. For twelve years I went to parochial school at St. Andrew's, and I guess I'm trying to find out if everything they taught me about God is true. And you're like a clean whiteboard that Juan is writing on—and helping you to write on too."

"So how would you classify yourself? Agnostic, theist, believer, or ...something else?"

"I'm definitely at least a theist. Before the plane crash I would have argued intensely that I'm a believing Christian. Now I think I'm a cultural christian who might be on her way to becoming an honest-to-God Christian. I still have some issues I struggle with though."

"Like what?"

"I have two major ones, and I don't know how to resolve either one. My sister Caroline did not fit Esperanza or Juan's description of a believing Christian. She assures me that the Bible teaches only believing Christians will spend eternity with God. I cannot accept the idea of Caroline suffering in Hell for eternity. Early on I thought that if Caroline is in Hell, then that's where I want to be too. Childish thinking, huh?"

"Very, but I think I understand."

"What about you, Adam?"

"My first issue is: 'God cannot be fair and just if he rescued me and let Caroline die.' A just and loving God would have rescued her and left me to die. I struggle with believing that God knows everything about me and still loves me so much that he spared me. And that even before he created everything and humans in his image, he knew we would rebel and need a savior—and he created us anyway!"

Adam said, "You said you have two struggles. What's the other one, Diana?"

"It'll take me a few minutes to explain it. About three months or so before Caroline met you, Adam, our Dad died. Caroline and I each received $17,500 inheritance. I had difficulty accepting the money, because I have long been convinced that it's morally wrong for a person to benefit from the death of another person."

"What connection does this have to do with your God-Quest today, Diana?"

"In at least two ways. I'm conflicted. I'm very attracted to you, Adam. But I think it would be morally wrong for me to benefit in any way from Caroline's death. So I feel I should reject any romantic feelings I have for you.

"I'm very interested in Juan's religious faith, and I'm happy that you're investigating Christianity. But I feel that I should not benefit from the death of Jesus—for me, that would be wrong. So I have this conflict between an attraction toward faith in God through Christ and equally a dislike of the idea. It's a constant, dynamic tension pulling me in opposite directions. What d'you think?"

"Honestly, I don't remember ever having those thoughts or feelings. So, at the moment, I have no response. Sorry. You should probably ask someone else."

Diana said, "I think I will, but maybe not Juan. At times, Juan's faith in God seems too radical. He repeatedly tells me that I should pray asking God to restore your memory. He dismisses my desire to pray for Caroline's salvation, he says it's too late. Do you think it's too late, Adam?"

"I don't know. Juan is very knowledgeable, and I'm sure he's a man of God. If God loves a piece of She-Yit like me, he must love Caroline infinitely more."

"Adam, please don't ever refer to yourself in those words again in my presence."

"Sorry. If you knew me much better, I fear you'd like me much less."

Privately, Diana called Rev. Noble and made an appointment to meet and discuss her questions and concerns. When seated in his office, she first reminded him that he'd helped Adam recently. Noble recalled that occasion and Adam. Then she repeated what she told Adam. "Rev. Noble, I've been listening to what Christian friends have said about Christianity, and I think I believe most, if not all, of what they say. But I've a couple of problems."

"Tell me about them."

"The first is this: I believe that it's morally wrong for a person to benefit from the death of another person. For instance, when my father died, my sister and I each inherited a modest sum of money. But I was troubled about receiving and spending that money, because I would be benefitting from the death of another person.

"I really like my late sister's fiancé, Adam, but I feel I should not have a loving, long-term relationship with him because I'd be benefitting from Caroline's death."

"And you're applying this value to Christianity?"

"Yes. How can I accept the death of Jesus on the cross as payment for my sins? I'd be benefitting from the death of another human—and I've long believed that's wrong, morally wrong."

"Well, you're overlooking two crucial points, Diana."

"I am? What are they?"

"First, Jesus was not only human, he was also divine—the unique Son of God."

"Yeah, I've thought of that. I'm not sure how that figures into the equation, but I doubt it changes the final answer. What's the second point?"

"This is the much more important, and it does change the final answer. True, Jesus died in your place, Diana, but he's alive!—the Father raised him to new life—and he wants you to accept his sacrificial atonement. Otherwise you are letting his death go to waste."

Diana was pensive and reflective for a moment. Slowly her facial expression changed from thoughtful to hesitant acceptance. "If I ignore his offer of forgiveness, that won't change the fact of his agonizing death by crucifixion or his resurrection—and he is alive! Yes. I'll focus on his being alive!

"Thanks, Rev. Noble. I think I'm already a Christian. I went to parochial school. I believe God really exists. What else do I have to do? Doesn't that make me a Christian?"

"Well, that's a good start, but simply believing that the one true God exists does not mean you're forgiven. In the second chapter of his letter, James wrote

"You believe that there is one God. Good! Even the demons believe that—and shudder.

"What else do I have to do besides believe there is one God?"

"We often use phrases like *receive Christ as your own Savior.* Let me explain what that phrase means.

"The New Testament teaches that a person must openly admit his or her disobedience to God, ask God to forgive her, and accept the death of Christ as the penalty for her sins. In this act, we commit ourselves to allowing God to rule our lives as both Savior and King. Would you like to do that, Diana?"

"I think I was doing that as you were explaining it to me. But I'm going to have to contemplate this for a day or two. I'll get back to you tomorrow or the next day. By the way, do you baptize converts?"

"Yes. Have you been baptized?"

"Yes. As a baby."

"How do you feel about that experience?"

"Of course, I don't remember it."

"Would you like to be baptized again?"

"I don't know. Should I?"

"We can talk about it. Do whatever God leads you to do."

"Thanks for helping me, I have to go now."

"Call me if you have any more questions, Diana."

"Please pray for Adam Bowers, and for God's will in our relationship."

"I do and I will. If you were convinced that God did not want you in a romantic relationship with Adam, would you break it off?"

"My mind says YES; but my heart says NO. How do I change my desire for relationship with God so that it's greater than my desire for intimacy with Adam?"

"You cannot do that alone, Diana. That'll require the power of God's Spirit in you."

"Why am I apprehensive, Rev. Noble?"

"Because you're dealing with an issue and a decision that has eternal consequences."

Diana left with her heart in turmoil. For the first few minutes she had an overwhelming desire to seduce Adam—even if it destroyed both of them. In the space of two seconds, Diana thought, *I'll go home and get in bed. If Adam does not come to my apartment, I'll call him and tell him that I'm sick; then he'll come. When he comes into my bedroom, I'll let the cover accidentally fall off and reveal my breasts. He won't be able to resist touching me. He'll lie down beside me and hold me.*

Immediately she thought, *Where the Hell did that come from? That's right, it came from Hell.* Then she spoke aloud and said, "God, I cannot change. Please change me"—and her feelings slowly began changing.

Sometime later, she became conscious of the fact that she was parked in her apartment complex, but she could not remember the drive home. The car's headlights were off, the engine was not running, and her face was wet with tears. With a heavy sigh, she exited the car and walked to the apartment door, thinking, *What just happened to me? How could I even think of something like this as I am so close to being baptized in Jesus' name?*

That Saturday evening at dinner, Adam suggested they visit a church on Sunday that Jackie had mentioned to him. But Diana had a different idea. "I'd like for you to go with me to Rev. Noble's church this Sunday morning."

"Biblical Community Church? Why do you want us to go there? Why this Sunday? We can go there any Sunday."

"Because I am to be baptized there this Sunday morning. And I really want you to be there."

Adam seemed mildly upset. "But Juan said a person should have a re-birth experience before he or she is baptized."

"Adam, look at me." She paused, "I have placed my faith in Christ."

"Huh? When? Why didn't you tell me?"

"I am telling you. I was hoping you'd notice a difference and ask me."

"Well, I'm speechless."

She smiled and said, "I guess that's just a side-benefit."

Diana was nervous as she dressed for church Sunday. She picked up her phone and called Adam. "Are you awake and getting dressed?"

He said, "Yes," but his voice sounded like he was still asleep in bed.

"Do you want me to drive?"

"No. I'll drive. I'll come get you. Can we get something to eat on the way? What time are you supposed to be there?"

"About nine-thirty or so."

"Why so early?"

"I think Rev. Noble wants to be sure that the people getting baptized understand what this means—and does not mean. He'll probably just repeat the printed instructions he mailed us earlier in the week."

When they entered BCC, an usher escorted them to the pastor's office. "Welcome, Diana, and Adam! I'm glad to see you again. I'm so glad you came with Diana. Will you stay here with us while I remind these few new converts what water baptism means—and does not mean?"

"If you don't think I'd be in the way."

"Not at all. Sit down, be comfortable. Do you want to be baptized today as well?"

"No. Not really. Maybe one day. Diana asked me to be here today."

"That's okay, I just wanted to be sure." After everyone had been introduced, Rev. Noble said, "As pastor, I like to be certain you each know what you are doing and what it means. Some Christian groups think baptism in water 'saves a person'. I do not believe that. I believe that many people been baptized and have not received God's forgiveness. On the other hand, there will certainly be some people with God in eternity who have never been baptized in water—like the thief on the cross next to Jesus.

"So why are new converts to Christianity today taught that they should be baptized in water? The short answer is simply this: our Master instructed us to be baptized. That should be enough for any Christian. But there's more. In water baptism a person symbolically experiences a personal death, burial, and resurrection—a restatement of what this person has already experienced spiritually and a proclamation of the gospel to the lost.

"In the New Testament new converts were baptized in public places like the Sea of Galilee or the Jordan River. Christianity is not a secret religion. In water baptism, a person is publicly confessing personal sin and proclaiming a commitment to trust Jesus as Savior and Christ as Ruler.

"We have separate private dressing rooms for ladies and for gentlemen. There should be someone in each of those dressing rooms to answer any questions you may have. Please remove your clothes—you may leave your underwear on if that will make you feel more comfortable. Find a clean dry white gown to put on.

"I will be in the baptistry water and call your name. At that time come down the steps and joined me in the water. If you would like to share a testimony just tell me, we have a microphone there—please do not touch it—just talk and everyone and everyone in the sanctuary will be able to hear you. If you're not comfortable testifying on your own, I will ask you these questions: 'Do you see yourself as a sinner in need of God's forgiveness?' If you do, you should answer 'Yes.'

"If you look at the congregation instead of me when you answer, the microphone will amplify your answer, and everyone will be able to hear you. Then I'll ask you, 'How have you received God's forgiveness?' You should answer, 'I am trusting in the death and resurrection of Jesus Christ'—or something very similar to that.

"At that point I will say something like, 'because of your confession of sin and your faith in the death and resurrection of Christ Jesus, I baptize you', then I will say your name, 'in the name of the Father, the Son, and the Holy Spirit.'

"When you come up out of the water, go back up the steps to your dressing room, find a clean, dry towel, and change back into your own clothes.

"At the close of the evening worship service, we will ask all of you to come down to the front of the auditorium, the deacons and the elders of the church will join me as we lay hands on you and pray that you will be faithful to the Lord Jesus."

Chapter 17: Searching in University Park

Rev. Parrish Wiseman said, "Adam, what would you like to ask me?"

"Tell me what your 'Aquarian Age Church' believes, Rev. Wiseman."

"Okay. Here's a summary. Because all religions will ultimately lead a person to God, we should respect all religions. But we are the only game in town that can teach you the 'deep mysteries' of Christianity."

"Oh, then you do believe the Bible."

"We read and discuss it, but I wouldn't say that we believe it. We don't consider it to be God's authoritative Word. But we can teach you the 'Deep Secrets' of faith in God.

"The Bible says little if anything about karma and reincarnation—two very important concepts to us. And parts of Hebrews seem to claim Christianity is superior to Judaism—a position we cannot embrace."

Even though he didn't have any confidence in anything Rev. Wiseman said, Adam felt it only fair to he ask Wiseman the same questions he asked all the other ministers. "Do you know God? Tell me how I can 'know God'."

Wiseman answered, "The three most important truths I've learned are these: "1. Because all religions lead to the same God, respect all religions; 2. Be faithful in living out whichever religion you embrace; and, finally, 3. Treat every living thing—both animals and plants—with love and respect because of karma."

Juan was upset and said, "Adam, if anyone tells you that they can teach you the deep spiritual secrets that only they know—you should stay away from them and continue reading the Bible."

"Juan, can you tell me the trick to getting God to answer my prayers? Of course, I mean to answer my prayer with YES and give me what I ask him for."

Juan said, "Adam, the disciples asked Jesus a similar question with They said 'teach us to pray.' He answered with what we call 'The Lord's Prayer,' and you can read it in Matthew 6 and Luke 11. Let me read it from Matthew in the Contemporary English Version, starting with verse 5.

When you pray, don't be like those show-offs who love to stand up and pray in the meeting places and on the street corners. They do this just to look good. I can assure you that they already have their reward.

When you pray, go into a room alone and close the door. Pray to your Father in private. He knows what is done in private, and he will reward you.

When you pray, don't talk on and on as people do who don't know God. They think God likes to hear long prayers. Don't be like them. Your Father knows what you need before you ask.

You should pray like this:

> Our Father in Heaven, help us to honor your name.
>
> Come and set up your kingdom, so that everyone on earth will obey you, as you are obeyed in Heaven.
>
> Give us our food for today.
>
> Forgive us for doing wrong, as we forgive others.
>
> Keep us from being tempted and protect us from evil.

"Juan, I like that translation. What is it?"

"The CEV. I just hope that you don't model your prayer life after what we often hear in many churches. First, prayer is often called 'two-way conversation' with God. Probably what God has to tell you is more important than what you have to tell God. So, many Christians read the Bible before, after, or during prayer.

"You do not need any flowery prayer. God understands all languages—earthly and heavenly. Don't try to impress people near you with your oratory skills. You're speaking to God, not to people—and God will not be impressed with your eloquence.

"You don't need to pray aloud or too long. You don't need to repeat yourself over and over and over again.

"You don't need to quote the Scriptures to God—he knows his promises better than you do.

"Don't try to use the name of Jesus to twist the Father's arm. The Father, the Son, and the Holy Spirit are all one. The name of Jesus is not a magical incantation, not an "Abracadabra," that we recite in order to

Steve Badger

SURVIVOR

manipulate God—nor is it a mantra we recite to conjure up God's Spirit. We should not use his name in vain.

"Don't think that the more people you get to pray with you, the more likely the Father is to grant your request.

"You don't really need to explain everything to God—he already understands your request better than you do.

"We don't convince God to give us what we ask for them by repeating his name or titles over and over again. Some people will say 'Father,' 'God,' 'Master,' 'Jesus,'' Lord,' 'Savior,' 'King,' 'Christ,' and other such names and titles over and over in prayer as if these will motivate him to give us what we ask for in prayer.

"It won't help to get famous TV preacher to pray with you. God will grant your request just as quickly as he will grant a request by Billy Graham.

"Fasting and praying in tongues may be good for the Christian, but they don't guarantee that God will grant your request.

"If you listen to people pray in church, you will probably hear all of these mistakes—but I hope you won't adopt them."

"I've heard many of them already in the churches I have visited. It may be part of what prompted me to ask you the question. Is that all?"

"Alas, no. I have at least two most important things to tell you about prayer. The New Testament teaches us that prayer is supplication. We *ask* God in prayer–we do not *tell* God in prayer. He is the King! We are his slaves! Never *command* God!

"So far, you've only told me mistakes to avoid, which is good, but I hope you also have something positive to tell me, Juan."

"I do, Adam, and it's very important, too. The only guarantee to answered prayer I've found in the Bible is to ask according to God's will and purpose. I think this is part of what it means to 'pray in Jesus' name.'

"God is faithful because that's his nature. God always answers our prayers. We should be just as thankful when his answer is 'No' or 'Later' as we are when his answer is 'Yes'.

"Christians do not have to try to 'talk God into' answering our prayers. He already wants to do more for us than we are asking and believing. Instead, we need to learn how to pray Spirit-led prayers that are 'in his will.' Only then will we see all our petitions granted."

More than once Juan encouraged Adam to read the Bible, especially the New Testament. He said, "You should experience the living Christ as you read the Bible." But Adam did not quite believe this and was not an ardent reader, so he was not completely faithful in regularly reading Scripture.

One evening he was feeling far from God, and he recalled Juan's counsel. He stared at a Bible that was across the room for a few moments, silently willing it to come to him. Finally he walked across the room, picked it up, and walked back to his recliner. Before opening the Bible, Adam silently prayed, *God, please direct me to a passage that will help me know you.* As he waited for God to speak to him, one idea repeatedly came to his mind: *Jesus was crucified for our sins.*

He consulted the concordance in the back of the Bible and then realized that he could read about the death of Jesus in Matthew, Mark, Luke, or John. *How do I choose the best account for me to read tonight? I'll read and compare all four of them!* He did just that, first in Matthew, then in Mark, Luke, and finally John. He read the four accounts of the resurrection of Jesus as well.

But after reading the gospel accounts of the crucifixion, Adam realized that he knew very little about what happened at a crucifixion—other than a wooden cross and someone died. So he did some online research. He also read about it in one of Juan's *Zondervan Pictorial Encyclopedia of the Bible* and rented *The Passion of the Christ* at a movie rental store. Adam was repulsed by the brutality of this ruthless method of execution.

He asked Juan, "Why did the God allow such a horrible execution of his Son?"

Juan replied, "For Jesus, the physical agony Jesus suffered on the cross was to communicate to us the spiritual agony he suffered by taking our sins on himself and having his Father abandon him."

Now Adam began to appreciate the *crown of thorns* they'd pressed on Jesus' head and the *nails* that pierced his hands. His rescue from the plane came to his mind: *the person who rescued me from the doomed airplane had scarred wrists and a scarred forehead.* He shouted, "Oh My God! I was right!"

Juan asked, "What is it, Adam?"

"The person who rescued me from the plane had scars on his forehead and on his wrists near his hands!"

Juan, "You saw the stigmata? Tell me more."

"He looked like a man, but he had the power of Almighty God, and somehow I knew that this was God."

Juan was still unaware that Adam knew that Juan was dying with cancer, and Adam urgently wanted to learn all he could from Juan before his life ended.

"Juan, does the Bible clearly tell us that we can know God? Or is it a doctrine that we compile from various Scriptures? Like we do for the doctrine of the Trinity."

"Tonight, read 1 John—near the end of the New Testament—in the NIV New Testament I gave you. Take a highlighter and highlight everything that short letter says about what we can know and how we can know it. Then, tomorrow evening, you and Diana come eat dinner with Esperanza and me at her home. Okay?"

"Sure. What time should we be there? 5:30?"

"Probably 6:00 or 6:30. Call me and we'll settle that."

"No problem. Juan, how would you answer the questions I've been asking ministers at area churches?"

"Please state them again."

"I've asked, 'Do you know God?' 'I want to know God. Can you tell me how to know God?' And here lately, I've had a third question: 'Can a person know that he knows God'?"

"I've started to answer those questions a few times, but something always distracted me. Instead of my trying to give you an answer right now, let's do this: before tomorrow evening, read 1 John, and let's discuss that short letter tomorrow night."

"Sounds good. Thanks."

That afternoon Diana received a call from Deputy Miller. "Ms. Norris, I just want to let you know that we've recovered your sister's handbag—and her cell phone was inside."

"Thank you, ma'am. Will you mail both to me?"

"Yes. But I wanted to tell you what else we discovered. We found a 'selfie' photo on her phone of the two of them—Caroline and Adam—in their seats on the plane. The time-date stamp on the photo puts it on the day of the crash, about 13 minutes after the plane left Love Field.

"Further, the face of the passenger sitting directly behind Caroline and Adam is easily identifiable in that picture. We no longer have any doubt. We now have physical proof that Adam was beside Caroline on that plane. We still have no idea how he escaped death. Has he told you anything that would help us answer that question?"

"No. He did say it was 'an act of God.' But for years, he's been a hard core, dyed-in-the-wool atheist, so I'm unsure what he means by that."

"Yeah. I don't think I'll suggest they include that in the official report. Thanks. I'll put her purse and phone in the mail to you today."

"Thank you."

"You're welcome."

Diana did not tell Adam the news of the photo that confirmed his surviving the plane crash until they left Juan and Esperanza that evening.

That night, Juan and Adam worked their way through 1 John, focusing on what John said could be *known*.

"What did you discover as you read 1 John, Adam?" Diana and Epseranza were very attentive as the two friends talked. They felt free to join the conversation, but were enthralled by the interaction of mentor and mentee.

"The writer just hammered on what we could know. He left little to doubt." Adam opened the NIV New Testament that Juan had given him weeks ago.

"So read to me what you highlighted."

"I did not find the word "know" until the 3rd verse of the 2nd chapter. I'll read it.

> "We know that we have come to know him if we keep his commands."

"True, but did you notice that the first chapter explicitly claims Christians have an experiential knowledge of God's Messiah, Jesus Christ?"

"I do now. The next few verses equate a knowledge of God and the love of God with an obedience to God's commands. Then John tells his readers that knowing God is expressed as love for people.

"In chapter 2, he states that young men, fathers, and children can all know God. He further states that believers know the truth—but I was not positive what truth he was making reference to."

"Probably to the Christ. The Gospels quote Jesus as saying, 'I am the way, the truth, and the life'...." And later in this letter, John refers to God as the one 'who is true'."

"In Chapter 3 he warns us that just as nonbelievers did not *know* Jesus, nonbelievers today will not *know* the children of God—but we believers can *know* that when Christ returns, we will become like him. Further, we can *know* that Christ came to take away our sins and that we will not just keep on sinning if we *know* him, because the children of God 'do what is right' and 'love brothers and sisters.'

"We *know* what 'love' is because Jesus demonstrated 'love' to us.

"We *know* that we know Christ because we love people."

"We *know* that Christ lives in us because his Spirit lives in us.'

"In the 5th chapter, John tells us that we can *know* that we have eternal life. Beyond that, we can *know* that he hears us when we pray, and he answers our prayers.

"Adam, do you realize that you skipped over some of the things John told us we could know?"

"I'm not too surprised."

"So what's your answer to the question? Can we know that we know God?"

"Well John's answer was a dogmatic 'Yes!' And I agree with John."

"Just be sure you remain humble. While we do have a personal, God-given knowledge of God, we Christians do not have all knowledge. And we should be quick to admit ignorance in areas that we do not have knowledge."

I think I'll re-read 1 John from a few other translations of the Bible."

"That should prove profitable, Adam."

Shortly after they left Juan and Esperanza to drive home, Diana told Adam about the phone call and the selfie photo, Adam was overjoyed. She asked, "Why is this so important to you, Adam?"

"People will no longer have any reason to doubt that I was on that plane. And I no longer have to question whether or not I had a real encounter with God. Without question, he rescued me—even if it was a mistake."

"It was no mistake, Adam."

Chapter 18: Shrink Wrapped Again

"Come in, Adam. Please be seated. I'll be with you in a moment. I have to finish my notes."

"Thanks, Dr. Bailey." Adam looked out the window until Dr. Bailey said, "Alright. I'm ready now. I think I see Diana later this week. How do you think she's doing?"

"She seems to be working through her grief more constructively than she was. Her nightmares are much less frequent now."

"Great. She is a very attractive young lady." He took a few minutes to scan over his notes from previous sessions with Adam.

"I received the email that you sent me yesterday with the attached photograph you took with Caroline's cell phone on the airplane. So we now have empirical evidence to substantiate your account of being on the plane that crashed—not that I ever doubted your testimony. I spoke with the McLennan County sheriff's office. They told me the source and history of the picture and affirmed its authenticity. Even though we cannot explain it, we now all agree that you were on the plane. What we don't know is how you escaped death and survived without even a scratch."

"All I lost was my luggage, my fiancée, and my memory."

"Are you regaining any memory?"

"Swiss cheese. Bits and pieces here and there, but not completely— mostly holes. I never lost some memory of Caroline. I barely recall the first few hours after the crash. I recall being at the hospital in Waco."

"Adam, would you tell me what you experienced in detail, please."

Adam removed a small object from his shirt pocket and said, "I want to record this so I don't have to repeat it for Diana, my mentor Juan, and friends at work. So I brought a Sony digital voice recorder. Is that okay?"

"That's fine. If you don't mind, I'd like to have my assistant transcribe it. Would you leave it with us for a few days so we can do that?"

"Sure. I'll try to put events in chronological order and describe things as they appeared to me at the time."

"And I will try hard to not interrupt you. Put this glass of water on the table next to you so if your mouth or throat gets dry, just pause and take a sip."

Adam closed his eyes and took a deep breath. "It was late afternoon when Diana took us to Love Field. Caroline and I each had a medium-sized suitcase on wheels. We went through security and waited to board the plane.

"Caroline sat next to the window, and I sat next to the aisle. We had a fifteen minute delay on the tarmac, and soon we cleared for take-off, and we were roaring down the runway and in the air. She was animated with anticipation. *In a few hours*, we thought, *We'll be in a nice hotel in Cancún where we'll spend the whole week.*

"Shortly after we reached cruising altitude, we hit some turbulence and fastened our seat belts. I'm a nervous flyer, so Caroline teased me about being afraid of flying. The captain spoke over the PA, apologizing for the rough flight and informing us that he was trying to fly above thunderstorm clouds. I could see black clouds and lightning below us. It was dark, both because night was falling and the clouds were blocking the last of the day's sunlight—until we got above the clouds.

"Then I heard a loud noise and the plane jarred as if it hit something—but there's nothing to hit at 32,000 feet up—or so I thought. Fear enveloped me. I was in a panic. I thought, *So this is how I will die.* I recall being upset because I could not recall the date or which day of the week it was. I have no idea why this was suddenly so important to me—but it was.

"I prayed! Me, an atheist! Prayed! I closed my eyes and whispered, "God, I never did find out if you really exist, but I guess I'm about to find out now." In a sense I was being dishonest when I'd tell people that I was searching for evidence of God's existence—dishonest because I'd already made up my mind that he did not exist. I was not really searching the way I claimed I was.

"When I opened my eyes, everything was dark and silent, as if I was deaf. I assumed we'd lost power and had no cabin lights. The plane felt like it was in free fall. Then I saw a tiny bluish light in front of me. That speck of light grew larger and larger until it filled the aisle beside me.

That reminds me, on the way to see you today, I had Sirius XM radio on in the car, listening to Christian music. Chris Tomlin was signing "How Great Is Our God," and one of the lyrics describing God was "He wraps himself in light…. That is a fair description of my experience."

"I heard a voice say, 'Now you know. Adam. I am.' The bluish light was too bright for me to look at directly. The voice said, 'stand up and follow me.' The voice sounded neither like that of a man or a woman, and it had no accent—but it was not like a computer-generated voice either. I am not positive it was a physical sound or just in my head.

"I unbuckled my seat belt, stood up—oblivious to my surroundings— and I was enveloped in that pale bluish light, as if in a cocoon, and it tightened around me. For the first time I could see a man in a long white robe next to me. But I could not see his whole face—just his forehead, which had many scars on it, as did his wrists, where they connected to the hand.

"The voice said, 'Don't be afraid.' I was about to say, 'I'm not afraid—which was not true—I was terrified. Before I could speak, at that moment, all fear evaporated. At first I could not see anything except that light around me. Then it was as if a fog lifted, and I saw the plane below me, falling to the ground. Because the sun had almost completely set, I barely saw the plane hit the ground, break apart, and one part of it burst into flame.

"Then I guess I passed out. Later—I don't know how long—I saw a man standing over me and shining a flashlight in my face and the light bluish light was gone. I tried to tell him to shut the flashlight off, but my mind was muddled and my speech was jumbled.

"I vomited once or twice. I cried to think that Caroline—the only beautiful part of my life—was gone. I kept thinking, *What just happened? Who am I? Who rescued me? What did the voice mean by saying 'Now you know, I am'*? People don't talk like this. I might say, 'Hi, I am Adam'. Or a repairman might say, 'I am here to fix your dishwasher' or 'I am finished,' or 'I am leaving.' No one says 'I am.' That's not a complete thought! *What's the rest of his sentence? 'I am* WHAT?

"I think you know the rest of this story, Dr. Bailey."

"Yes. Tell us what you've been doing since the accident, Adam."

"I've been trying to find out who I was and determine who I will become. Caroline's sister, Diana, has been helping me find my way around. We have worked to avoid becoming romantically involved—but our success at that may be coming to an end.

"I have no explanation other than God rescued me from that plane before it crashed. I know that this explanation is as preposterous to most people as it would have been to me before the accident. Since then, I have sincerely searched to find who rescued me—I'll call him or it God for the time being anyway."

"Why are you searching only in Christianity? Did you grow up in a Christian home?"

"Not really. Truth be known, possibly primarily because we live in a country with a Judeo-Christian history. But, equally candid, Christianity is the only religion that has anything in common with my experience. I've read a little about some non-Christian religions and do not find as much consistent with my experience."

"What are the features of your experience that you find harmonious with Christianity?"

"Much of what I've learned about Christianity comes from reading most of the New Testament a few times in the past few weeks, visiting half a dozen churches and talking with their ministers, and the opinions of Juan Reyes, a close Christian friend and a trusted spiritual mentor.

"Juan tells me that, in the book of Exodus, the God of the Bible told Moses to tell the Pharaoh of Egypt that 'I AM' sent him. This is what the person who rescued me said, 'Now you know. I AM.' This narrowed my search down to the three 'Abrahamic Faiths': Islam, Judaism, and Christianity.

"Juan showed me in John's Gospel, the fourth New Testament book, that some people said that Jesus was possessed by a demon, and Jesus responded by telling them that Abraham saw his day. People answered him by saying, 'You're not even 50 years old, and you claim to have seen Abraham?' Jesus told them, 'Before Abraham was born, I AM.' He did not say 'I WAS—which would have made more sense to me. He said, 'I AM.' I didn't see it, but Juan pointed out to me that the people who heard him thought he had blasphemed by calling himself I AM. If Jesus of Nazareth is not God in human flesh, then he was guilty of blasphemy.

"Later I did some research on the crucifixion. The person in the bluish light cocoon who rescued me had scars on his forehead and on his wrists near his hands."

"So you think the God of the Bible sent Christ Jesus to rescue you from the plane?"

"Now you know why I've hesitated to tell anyone what I've experienced. I don't want to spend the rest of my natural life in an insane asylum. If you had my experience, how would you interpret it, Dr. Bailey?"

"I have no idea."

"So, am I dangerous? Do I need to be committed to a mental institution?"

"No more dangerous than the millions of other people who think the Bible is divinely inspired, I guess," he said with a condescending smile.

"What about you, Dr. Bailey? Have you placed your faith in the death and resurrection of Jesus Christ?"

"I would have said yes, but in light of your experience, I guess the truthful answer is no."

Adam left his digital voice recorder with Bailey's secretary. A few days later, Adam received a letter from Dr. Bailey. In the envelope, he found his recorder and a transcript of his testimony that he'd recorded. The next day, he photocopied it and mailed a copy to Gary and Sherry, a copy to Juan, and another to Rev. Noble.

Within a week, four area Pentecostal ministers invited Adam to give a testimony one Sunday morning to their congregation. At first he was awed, then a little nervous, and then flattered. The next time he saw Juan, he told him of the invitations and asked for his advice.

"Can you testify about what God has done in your life in a way that makes him the hero of the story? Or will you tell them what happened in a way that glorifies you, Adam?"

"There's a difference?"

"Yes. Maybe you should postpone this until you know that you have had a genuine conversion experience—and you are more mature in your faith."

Chapter 19: His Quest Ends in Death

Adam's cell phone rang, and he saw that it was Juan. "Hey, Juan, what's up *amigo*?" It was Juan's phone, but it wasn't Juan.

"Adam. It's Esperanza. Juan is in ICU at Presbyterian Hospital in Dallas. He told me to call and ask you to come visit him as soon as possible. Can you come today?"

"I'm on my way right now. Are you there with him now?"

"Yes." Adam hung up and immediately called Diana, "Juan is in ICU at Presbyterian. I'm on my way there now. Esperanza is with him."

"Can you come get me on your way?"

"I'm three minutes from your apartment. Are you ready?"

"Yes. Sound the horn and I'll come out."

Adam did not have to sound the horn—Diana was watching out a window, and she was out the door and in the car before the vehicle stopped.

"Don't drive like a maniac, Adam."

"You sound just like Caroline. Right?"

Diana was surprised. "Exactly! Did you remember that?"

"No. Just guessed. Do you want to drive?"

"Yes, please!" After they switched places, she asked, "Oh. What did Esperanza say on the phone."

"Just that he's in ICU at Presbyterian and asking us to come see him."

"Adam, do you think he's dying now?"

"Well, if the doctors are right, he should have at least one or two more weeks. This may happen a few more times before the end, Diana."

As they walked into the hospital, she asked, "Do you think I should go into ICU with you? Or should I stay in the waiting room?"

"Come in to ICU. Juan and Esperanza really like you."

"You don't know if she likes me."

"Why else would she have confided in you at her wedding? Of course she likes you. Everyone likes you.

"Even you, Adam?" By now they had left the elevator and were walking down the hall toward ICU.

"You know that I love you, Diana? Why do you even ask?"

"You love me as you would love a kid sister."

"And...?"

"I want you to love me as an adult woman. I want you to think of me amorously, romantically—not platonically. I don't want to have a filial relationship with you." Diana knew that Esperanza had privately helped her to realize her love for Adam did not dishonor Caroline—she was just agreeing with her evaluation of Adam.

"Caroline." He said, "Caroline" with no inflection, as if it were a complete sentence. And Diana knew precisely what he meant. *Will he ever be over Caroline?*

"Yes. I want you to process your grief over Caroline and move on to feel some of those same feelings for me. Is that possible?"

"I'm not sure. Maybe. Time will tell. Right now I'm totally focused on Juan's illness, recovering my memory, and deciding if God does or does not exist—I cannot be romantic too."

Right. Poor timing on my part. Sorry. But now you know how I feel, Adam. They were at the door to ICU when she finished her thought out loud. "I love you, Adam." She would have kissed him, but the nurse opened the door to ICU for them at that very moment.

The nurses led them into the small room where Juan seemed to be sleeping. He had an IV in his left arm and wires connected to him and to instruments monitoring his vital signs. His back was to them. They stood silently for a moment, and were about to speak, when Juan said, "Thank you for coming, Diana."

"How did you know I was here?"

"That fragrance you're wearing—even though it's a little strong, I like it. It preceded you and shouts, 'Diana's here!'" This made her feel a little self-conscious. "I hope Adam's with you."

She said, "He is" at the same time he said, "I am." Juan chuckled, but did not open his eyes or roll over to face them.

"Diana, thanks for coming to see me. I'm glad Adam came with you." Then they noticed Esperanza sitting in a darker corner of the room. She dried her eyes and greeted each of them with a hug. "I'm so glad you're both here with us."

Adam turned back to the bed, "Can we pray and tell God to heal you?"

Juan chuckled, "Adam, nobody tells God what to do. Nobody. He's God, not Santa Claus or the tooth fairy! He's the King of kings and Lord of lords. God almighty! The Creator. You'd sooner use a cooked limp spaghetti strand to give a wildcat an enema than to tell God what to do!" *Where does he come up with these bizarre metaphors?* Adam wondered silently.

"I meant, can we ask God to heal you?"

"Yes, we can. And for the past several weeks, Esperanza and I have been asking. But God has shown both of us that my departure is near. So I've stopped asking him to heal me, and just asked that he would accomplish his will and purpose in my life and my death."

"That's magnanimous, Juan, but I need you to help me finish my quest. How can I gain faith in God without you, *amigo?* Surely God knows this!"

"I have no doubt that you will, Adam. You've been on a faith-trajectory ever since God rescued you from the plane crash. You don't need me anymore. You probably have not noticed it, but when we first met, you just believed anything I said about God. But as your knowledge of God and your knowledge of Scripture have increased, you've been slower to just accept anything I say. Your critical thinking about God has been maturing—and this is as it should be.

"You never really needed me, Adam—it was I who really needed you."

"What do you mean? How did you need me?"

"You forced me to rehearse the foundations of my faith in God at a time that I most needed to be reminded of them—although I did not realize it. Soon you will place your trust in the Messiah Jesus."

"Who will teach me when you're gone, Juan?" Adam smiled as he noticed the assonance in 'gone Juan.'

"God's Spirit will teach you from His Word—as he has been doing for several weeks. I can point people to him, but he alone is the one who draws people to himself and reveals himself. You'll see. He will lead you into truth—all truth."

"Juan, you are the best revelation of Christ that I have ever known."

"Oh Adam, I'm such a poor imitation of the Messiah. He is so much greater than I."

"What can I do for you, *amigo?* Why did you ask me to be here?"

"I want you to be here and experience my death with me."

"Oh, great. Thanks for this 'act of kindness'." Adam's sarcasm was obvious. "Please don't do me any favors. What the" he paused, then continued "Heaven were you thinking?"

"It really is an act of kindness. If you experience this with me, you'll lose your fear of dying. I will no longer be here with you, Adam, but Scripture teaches us that I will be present with the Lord. Being here with me tonight will be like graduation or a new beginning—for both of us. Perhaps my death will bring you to a fuller knowledge of God."

"In that case, I don't want to miss it." After a brief pause, he said, "Do you have any regrets, Juan?"

"A few. After I'm gone, Esperanza will give birth to our son. I regret that I won't know him and be involved in his life. And she'll have to go through her difficult 'grief work' without me. Maybe Diana will be her support, comforting her with the comfort that God gave her when Caroline died.

"Also, I won't be physically present when you're baptized in water."

"Oh, I could be baptized tonight, right now, in a bathtub. You could baptize me."

"Adam, I told you before, the New Testament pattern is for water baptism to take place *after* the person has been reborn. When you're ready to be baptized in water, find a public place and invite everyone you know—Christian and non-Christian—to come and witness it. Don't be baptized hidden away in a semi-private church baptistery."

"We could switch that, right? And you could baptize me tonight."

"Maybe we could, but I won't. I do appreciate your generous gesture. I'm tired. Would you just sit with me while I sleep?"

"Juan, I still don't know why God spared me. What purpose does he have for me? I need to find an answer to that question."

"Don't worry about it. Just take one step at a time, and trust him. Now I'm tired and must nap."

"Okay. But don't die yet."

"I'll try not to."

A few minutes later Juan asked, "Adam, what will you do with the money in the shoebox in the safe?" Diana had been talking with Esperanza, but their conversation was over, and she heard this question. Money? What money? Did the small box in the safe have cash in it? She did not turn her head, but she tuned in to hear Adam's answer. He spoke so quietly she could barely hear him.

"I've thought of lots of solutions. I know cannot keep it. I've thought of giving it to a church or charity—but they might reject the gift if they knew what it is. I've thought of going to the IRS and just telling them what it is, pay the tax and the penalty—but I've no confidence in government bureaucrats—and the thought of going to prison has no attraction to me. What do you think I should do, Juan?"

"I won't say 'You do the crime; you do the time.' I don't have any advice—except, do whatever God's Spirit directs you to do. You cannot just trust your conscience!"

"True."

"Adam, what are you going to do about her?" Juan looked in Diana's direction as he said "her." Diana was listening even more closely to this conversation.

"I'm not sure what'll happen. Why?"

"You do know that she's in love with you, right?"

"I just found out as we came into ICU. How did you find out?"

"Esperanza told me that she has been noticing Diana's interaction with you—and I think she's right."

"What do you think I should do, Juan?"

"Wait until you have had a genuine rebirth experience, find out all that the Bible teaches about marriage, and then follow God's leading. And don't have sexual intercourse before you're married."

"Yeah, I'll try to do that. We have avoided sexual intimacy so far, but I can tell that we're headed in that direction."

After a silent moment, Esperanza said, "Juan, I brought the Eucharist. Our pastor teaches that only Christians should eat The Lord's Supper. What should we do?"

"Oh, we can leave the room so you two could be alone," Adam said.

Diana joined in the offer, "Yes. Why don't we give you two a few minutes of privacy."

Adam said, "Hey, wait a minute. Diana's a Christian—she was baptized last Sunday."

Juan and Esperanza both spoke at the same time with the same request, "What! Why didn't you tell us? How did you come to faith, Diana?"

"I was hoping someone would notice the difference and ask me. I've been listening to all of y'all tell about God's love for us, and I've been watching Adam as he searched to find the truth.

"I had counseled with Rev. Noble, telling him about my issues with Christianity, and he helped me to see how trusting in Christ affirms his sacrifice on the cross.

"I was trying to fall asleep a few nights ago, and I realized that I was a sinner. So, I spoke aloud, 'God, I have a sinful nature and I've done sinful things. If you're really real, let me experience the forgiveness that Juan and Esperanza say they've experienced.' And God changed me."

"In what way did God change you? What happened?"

"I went right to sleep. I slept all through the night, with no bad dreams. The next morning as I was waking up, I realized that I was different, and I said, "God, thank you for forgiving me. Let me learn how to serve you." Then it was if God gave me a hug that said, "I love you, my child," and I said, "I love you, Lord Jesus." I had already spoken with Rev. Noble, and I've asked him if I could be baptized."

Juan said, "I know Adam is about to come to faith too. But Adam, you should not respond to pressure from us. Just be obedient to God. God's timing is always perfect."

Then Juan saw the bread and wine, and he turned to Adam and said, "My friends, God invites everyone to his table. No one is to be turned away. Maybe our celebration of the presence of Christ Jesus in The Lord's Supper will take on new meaning for all of us, and you won't regret joining us in proclaiming the crucifixion of Jesus with us. Years from now, Esperanza will weep as she recalls your participation with us. It will be your first act of faith and hope."

Esperanza mumbled, "I'm crying now, *mi querido*."

She opened the plastic bowl with some unleavened bread and produced a small bottle of wine, but they had only one glass, a plastic hospital glass. Each one of them took a small piece of bread and looked at Juan.

Juan explained the significance of this celebration to them. "On the night that the Lord was betrayed, he ate a Seder meal, the Passover with his disciples. That Jewish custom commemorated what God did to persuade the Pharaoh to free the Israelites from slavery in Egypt and precipitated the

Exodus. But that night God gave it a new meaning. Jesus of Nazareth was about to become the Passover Lamb and offer forgiveness to all people.

"Paul wrote that this unleavened bread now symbolizes the body of Jesus, who died on the cross for our sins." Each of them put a piece of the hard unleavened bread into his or her mouth, and Juan prayed, "Father, thank you for sending Jesus to live and die for our sins. Jesus, thank you for being obedient to the Father—even to the point of dying painfully on the cross for our sins."

Diana and Adam watched Juan, and as he put the bread in his mouth, they also put their bread in their mouths. When he said, "Thank you, Lord Jesus," they said, "Thank you, Lord Jesus."

"Then Jesus took the cup of wine and said, 'This is the new covenant in my blood, which is poured out for you'." Again, when Juan drank the wine, he handed it to Esperanza, she handed it to Diana, and she handed it to Adam. Sequentially, they each drank some of the wine.

When Juan said, "Thank you, Lord Jesus," they all said, "Thank you, Lord Jesus."

Adam and Diana knew that this was a very sacred moment and were appropriately reverent. With the taste of the wine still in his mouth, Adam's eyesight blurred. He tried to talk but could not make a sound. He wiped his eyes, but he was not crying, and that did not improve his eyesight. Then he noticed a tiny bluish light—about the size of a candle flame—near Juan. And Adam knew that the same person who rescued him from the plane crash was doing something inside of him now.

Juan sat up in bed, looked at Adam and said, "My brother, God has already revealed himself to you, and you know he exists. What prevents you from confessing your sins and asking God for his forgiveness? Why do you hesitate to trust him and commit your life to him?"

"I've always felt like I was in control of my life, and I don't want to surrender control of my life to anyone. What if God wants me to be a missionary or to give all of my financial investments to charities? I'm not sure what God would require of me. What if he wants me to marry a fat, ugly, witch-woman?"

"True. God will demand your complete allegiance and submission to his will—not lip-service. He will own you; you must become his slave. What will you do, my friend? Can you trust God?"

"I will give him everything—my sinful nature and sinful actions. My plans for the future, my sexual desires, my money, my business, my friendships, everything. I'll trust him with my life."

"Will you trust him with your death as well?"

Adam hesitated as he thought, then said, "I'm really not sure I have the strength to do that, Juan. But I'll try."

"Then trust his Spirit to make you strong. God is all-powerful."

"By his grace, I'll trust him with life and with death."

As if a searchlight entered the room, the small bluish light filled the room with a bright blinding light as Juan spoke. "*Mi hermano* Adam, The time for my departure is here. I'm leaving. I will see you when you join me. Every day tell my wife how I love her and tell my son how I long to have him join us with *el Salvador*—will you teach him, Adam?"

"I will, my brother. And we will take care of your wife and son as if they were my own children. We will give them a home and provide for their needs, as God blesses my business. I make this vow to you in the presence of God."

A loud noise startled Adam. "Did you hear that, *Hermano*? God is speaking to us!"

"It sounded like thunder to me, *amigo.*"

"You heard thunder. I heard God say, *'Un momento, mi hijo.* I tell you, Adam, you better learn Spanish—that's what we'll all be speaking in Heaven."

"I still say it sounded like thunder."

The bright light beside Juan that blinded Adam slowly dimmed, and now Adam could see it was a person dressed in a brilliant white robe. The person looked at Juan and said, "I've been sent to escort you into His Presence."

And Juan said, "I'm ready."

Adam said, "Well I'll be Dav-Yim'd. No wings."

Juan turned to him and said, "No. Don't ever say that you will be damned, Adam. Say you will be forgiven."

"Yes, I will be forgiven. I am forgiven."

When Adam said this, three things happened simultaneously: Juan fell back and took his last breath; the heart monitor alarm screamed; Adam collapsed on the floor; and the bluish light grew dimmer and dimmer until it disappeared.. Immediately Esperanza ran to the bed shouting, "Juan!" Nurses ran into the room to shut off the alarm. And Diana almost panicked as she tried to detect signs of life in Adam.

Esperanza held Juan's head in her lap and cried, "Goodbye my dear husband. I will join you soon." In spite of knowing that Juan would die soon, this moment caught Esperanza off guard, and she immediately missed him.

Adam quickly regained consciousness, but it took thirty minutes or more for that portion of ICU to return to its routine. Esperanza stayed with Juan until his body was removed almost an hour later by people from a nearby funeral home. Adam asked Esperanza for permission to make arrangements at the same funeral home in Plano that handled Caroline's funeral, and she agreed.

As he was about to leave, he took Diana aside and quietly said, "God has restored my memory."

"Completely?"

"I think so. We can test it later.'

Diana said, "Do you recall the name of your favorite high school teacher? "

"Mrs. Alice Boyd, English teacher."

"What was your father's middle name?"

"Langston."

"What's your Social Security Number?"

When Adam rattled off nine numbers with no hesitation, Diana said, "You can tell me the rest later. I'm riding with Esperanza—I'm driving her car, and she's ready to go."

"Good."

Adam drove home by himself—this was the first time he drove alone since the accident. As he drove home, he talked nonsense to the landscape. "Yes, I remember that building. Hello hotel. I've been missing you, Entrance to the North Dallas Turnpike. My memory is fine. Thank you, God! Memory, I've missed you! Welcome back."

Diana insisted that Esperanza sleep at Diana's apartment for at least one night; she stayed three nights.

After Juan's funeral, Adam worked on two projects. On Monday morning, he asked Tina and Skip to step into his office. He closed the door and told them, "I have a few things to tell you and a couple of questions." Skip immediately became extremely tense, dreading to hear what he imagined Adam would say.

"First, my memory is back—and I'm euphoric!"

Skip and Tina immediately called for a celebration. Skip braced himself and said, "And, item number two?"

"I'm in the process of converting to Christianity. Tina, I would like for you and Jackie to create a formal, official invitation to send to everyone we know—former clients, family, friends, enemies, competitors, stock holders, contractors, everyone," here he paused and handed her a post-it note.

"An invitation to what?"

"My festive public testimony of my conversion to Christianity, including a dinner party. I wrote down the date and times for the dinner. RSVP to you or Jackie. I'll give you a list of names and address of people to invite.

"Since the meal will be catered by one of Plano's best BBQ restaurants, we must have an accurate head count. At the end of the meal, Rev. Noble will baptize me in the pool, after that, I'll tell everyone a little about what brought me to faith in Christ. I have reserved the pool, the gazebo, and the entire recreation area at my condo complex for this gala. No gifts allowed. I promise, this is not a preaching event, just a meal and a baptism. Guests are welcome to bring a swimsuit for a swim party afterwards. If you have any problems putting together an invitation, call me and I'll advise."

"Adam, who's paying for the food? TR or you?"

"I am. Do you have another question?"

"Yes. Am I required to attend?"

"No one is required. But I'll be hurt if anyone at TR—including and especially you, Skip—refuse to attend. The whole event should take much less than an hour. Anyone needing to do something else that night should be free by six-fifteen or six-thirty at the latest, but they'll miss free food."

Adam asked, "Tina, do we have an opening for an onsite manager at any of our apartment complexes?"

"Yes. I'm looking for someone right now. Why?"

"I'd like for you and Jackie to train Esperanza Reyes for the job. She will be introduced at my baptism. I'm asking you two to do extra work for her first three months of on-the-job training—to be sure she is well-trained and does a good job. We'll have to work with her—she thinks she's pregnant. I'll pay you both a bonus at the end of her six- month probation period. If she does a good job for a year, we'll consider letting her work here in the office as the supervisor over all of our on-site managers. But don't tell her that."

"Please tell me she's bilingual."

"She is. You have been asking me for months to take this load off of you and Jackie, and now I'm working TR toward that goal."

"Hey, your memory really is restored!"

Skip asked, "Will she receive the same remuneration as our other on-site managers?"

"The same—unless you think that is not enough."

"No. That's fine."

Chapter 20: Baptism Celebration

Adam answered his cell phone, "Hello."

"Hi Mr. Bowers, this is Tina. We have a draft of the invitation to your dinner celebration for you to look at. Will you be in the office this morning?"

"Yes. Thanks. I'm on my way now. I'll be there in five or ten minutes. Good-Bye."

Adam had only a couple of suggestions to make to the invitation—simple changes that Tina accomplished in a dozen keystrokes and mouse maneuvers. He wanted the invitation to inform people that he is over his amnesia.

"Here's my list of names and addresses to add to what you have. How many people are we inviting?"

"Almost 300. With this list of names, maybe 325."

"So maybe 200 will come. Keep an accurate count of those who RSVP positively. Have it printed on a heavy ivory paper, like a wedding invitation, and include a stamped, addressed return envelope so it's easy for folks to reply."

"Have you contacted the caterer, given them a menu, and acquired a price?"

"Yes sir, and it won't be cheap."

"I know. But it'll be good."

As an owner of his condo, Adam could reserve the lodge, the pool, and the recreation area, but it cost a hundred dollars, required a deposit, and had to be reserved at least two weeks in advance. The complex had a separate parking lot for the Lodge. Guests began arriving around 5:40 pm. Some were dressed in a suit and tie, a few came wearing jeans and cowboy boots, and others came in shorts or swimsuits. The lodge was filled to overflowing. A bluegrass band played and sang through the meal.

At 5:45 p.m., the band played "The Yellow Rose of Texas," and everyone stood. Then they sang "Dixie," followed by "God Bless America," and finally the National Anthem. Of course, all of the guests sang along with them.

Then Adam stood at the microphone and said, "Thank you for coming, friends. Wasn't that meal great?" The applause, shouting, and whistles lasted several minutes.

"I'm glad you liked it. Thank you friends and family for coming to hear me publicly tell you what I've experienced these past few months. As a child I had no one to teach me about God's love for me. I never went to church. As a nineteen year old boy, I married my sweetheart, Sherry. Sherry, you and Gary, please stand. The crowd applauded wildly. "Sherry and I had a baby, but that baby died—and we pretty much blamed each other and God, and finally divorced. Before we split, Sherry provided the capital to open 'Terry Realtors,' and she still owns five percent of the stock in it—we thank her every three months by sending her a dividend check.

"While I was in school at UT in Austin," he had to pause while many guests shouted out "Go Longhorns" and "Bevo!" the name of the UT mascot. Adam patiently waited, then continued.

"At UT, I became an outspoken atheist. I also made friends with Skip Masters, still one of my best friends and business partners. Skip, are you here?" He heard someone yell, but he could not tell if it was Skip or someone else, and he never saw Skip—so he continued and assumed that Skip had skipped.

"Recently I fell in love with a Texas Belle named Caroline Norris, a nurse. I asked her to marry me, and she agreed." Someone in the crowd shouted, "What was she thinking?" provoking sustained laughter. Adam waited for the crowd to quiet down. Then he said, "Some of you know that a few months ago Caroline and everyone else on that plane died in the crash just south of Waco—everyone, that is, except me." The person who shouted "What was she thinking?" was mortified.

Now the crowd became very quiet, almost reverent. "At first, some people did not believe I was ever on that plane, but we have irrefutable proof that I was. How did I escape? My answer to that question will not satisfy some of you, but I was there, and I know what happened.

"God—the same God that I told everyone did not exist, rescued me. This revelation of God—and the death of Caroline—so overwhelmed me that for months my brain refused to allow me to remember most of my life. I could not even recognize pictures of my late parents or pet dog!

"But this amnesia and tragedy motivated me to try to find God. Caroline's sister, Diana, helped me and joined me in this God-Quest. I visited six or seven churches and interviewed several ministers, asking them 'Do you know God?' and 'Tell me how I can know God.'

"God provided a mentor in Juan Reyes, a brilliant, humble mentor to guide me to faith in Jesus of Nazareth, God's Messiah. This event tonight is just a venue for me to stand and tell you that I am now a follower of Christ Jesus. His Holy Spirit has changed me. I am committed to living for him in every way.

"And tonight, Rev. Noble will baptize me in water as a sign that I freely choose to put my will to death and allow God's Spirit to create a clean heart in me.

"So please meet me around the pool in three minutes and witness Rev. Noble baptize me. Please stay off the diving board and out of the water. If any of you wants to swim, please wait until the baptism is over. If any of you wants Rev. Noble to baptize you here tonight, talk to him now while I get into my white slacks and shirt. See you at the pool."

The pavement around the pool was packed with at least a couple of hundred friends and spectators by the time Adam walked into the water at the shallow end, meeting Nobel in chest-deep water. Nobel raised his hand and the crowd quickly became silent. Without any electronic amplification, Nobel's voice carried over the crowd.

"Adam Bowers, do you recognize yourself as a sinner?"

"I do. But I accept the death and resurrection of Jesus Christ as the payment for my sins."

"Are you willing for God's Spirit to help you put your will to death daily, and allow his Spirit to control your life?

"With God's help, I will."

"Adam Bowers, as an ordained minister of the Gospel, I baptize you in the name of the Father, the Son, and the Holy Spirit. May God empower you to fulfill your vow."

Some of the group did not hear the second sentence, because the crowd went wild with shouting when Adam's head went under the surface of the water, which was just as Rev. Nobel began to say "May God empower you...."

While he was under the water, Adam silently prayed, *Father, please let Juan know that I have been baptized.*

Chapter 21: Meeting with Skip

Two weeks after Juan's funeral, Esperanza began a week of training to become the onsite manager at an apartment complex owned and managed by TR.

Tina said, "As the on-site manager, you are responsible to interview and screen applications, receive rent, call repairmen, and other assorted minor duties. Your rent and utilities are paid, and you will be paid a modest income.

"Once a renter is moved in, you're the person they go to with problems. Here's a list of the plumbers, electricians, and other repairmen that TR uses. I've written them telling them that you are the complex onsite manager.

"Any problem you cannot solve, just call me or Jackie, and we will try to help you find a solution.

"Here's a little booklet that outlines the laws that govern the legal rights of 'the leaser and the lessee.' As the legal agent for TR, you must know what we can and cannot do—according to the state law.

"Esperanza, if you do this job well, one day you may move up to another position at Terry Realty that pays better." Esperanza did not forget this comment.

"Thank you Tina, for all of your help. What should I call Adam?"

"I don't think he cares. Except for Skip, all of us call him 'Mr. Bowers,' especially in front of a client.

"Every organization has a 'chain of command.' You work directly under me. If you have a problem, call me, if anyone else in the company tells you to do something, be polite, but tell me. Be helpful, but sales people should not tell you what to do. If you have a problem, do not go to Mr. Bowers to solve it, come to me. Unless I am the problem, in which case, you may go to Mr. Bowers, but you would be kind to me if you told me first and gave me a chance to correct the problem.

"Of course, Mr. Bowers is the Boss, and what he decides is what will happen, but he's an easy boss to work with. And he listens to subordinates—or at least, he used to before the plane crash.

"Jackie will show you the forms we use for prospective tenants. You do not have the authority to modify or ignore the payment of rent—either in date due or amount. If you are caught doing either, you will be fired.

"Jackie and I promise you that we'll do all we can to help you succeed, Esperanza. Any questions?"

"Is there a bus that goes between here and the apartment complex?"

"No. But that reminds me. Adam told me to give you these and tell you to use his Mercedes until he's able to help you find a car suitable for your transportation needs." With that, she handed Esperanza a set of car keys.

Adam said, "Skip, come talk to me for a few minutes, please."

"Sure." The two of them sat across a small table in a small conference room at TR.

"Is your memory completely restored?"

"Yes, it seems to be—with maybe one or two minor missing pieces. I remembered some gray areas in TR's business that I want us to change. Since you're the Sales Manager, I want you to help me implement them. I know that we've pushed the NAR ethical standards to the edge. Do you know what I'm talking about, Skip?"

"I'm not sure."

"Let me be a little more direct, and I hope you don't require me to be bluntly specific. If you pretend you don't understand me, I'll be forced to conclude that I cannot trust you.

"At times we—you and I—have turned a blind eye and deaf ear to monetary exchanges that were at least questionable—if not unethical or illegal. From now on, we will adhere strictly to NAR ethical procedures. Agreed?"

Skip started to justify their past actions, but he paused, sighed, and said, "Agreed."

"Can I trust you to communicate this in a clear, kind, but firm way to all sales persons?"

"Yes, you can."

"In order to accomplish this, I want you to assemble our sales force once a week in this conference room. I want you to work through the NAR's ethical standards explaining what each means and citing examples. This will be an in-house seminar."

"I can do that."

"I will be at these meetings too, but you will lead them. I probably need a refresher as much or more than any of our sales people. Let's start in two weeks. What's the best day and time for you, Skip?"

"Probably Tuesday or Thursday."

"Okay. Pick one. Can we say 4:00 until 5:30 p.m.?"

"Too many salesmen will be meeting clients at that time. How about 7:00 until 8:30 p.m.?"

"Talk to the sales people and see what they say. And let me know. How many meetings will you need?"

"It will take a total of four or five hours to cover, I think, depending on how much discussion we have. Should we try to cover it in one marathon session?"

"No. Spread it out over three to five weeks. Provoke discussion. Get our team to buy into the NAR ethical standards."

"Okay."

A knock at the door broke the silence, and Adam said, "Come in, Tina."

"Your attorney is on the phone, Mr. Bowers."

"Thanks, Tina. Please tell him I'm in a meeting and I'll call him back in a few minutes."

"Yes sir."

"Thank you, Tina."

"What's this, Adam?" Skip picked up a brownish-white engraved irregularly-shaped object about the size of man's wallet from Adam's desk. "And where did you get it?"

Adam answered the second question first. "Caroline and I found it on the beach in Oregon several months ago. It's probably whalebone—a piece of scrimshaw."

"Did you do the engraving? The ship is breathtaking!"

"Of course not. I cannot carve a Thanksgiving turkey. It was already engraved when we found it."

"The artwork is fantastic and detailed. You found this on a beach?"

"Yes. On the southern Oregon coast, between Harbor and Gold Beach—just north of California. Caroline saw it first."

"Have you ever tried to get an artist to speculate about which artist who carved this piece? Have you ever asked an appraiser to place a value on it?"

"No. My guess is that probably no one carved it. That engraving was produced by the sand and the waves of the oceans—and probably by some of the marine life, like barnacles, too."

Skip raised his voice a few decibels. "Adam, that's preposterous, absolutely ludicrous. Why would you suggest such an absurd, ridiculous provenance for this exquisite piece? Of course someone with great artistic talent planned this and carved the artwork with a very sharp tool."

With that, Skip put the piece of scrimshaw back on Adam's desk. As soon as Skip leaned back in his chair, Adam put a pale skeleton of a sand dollar beside it.

Still speaking quietly he said, "Skip, why do you insist that an intelligent, skillful agent produced that piece of scrimshaw," he pointed to the scrimshaw and then to the skies as he continued, "but the billions of galaxies, our solar system, and our planet Earth," without pausing he pointed to the sand dollar, "with its great variety of life—infinitely more complex than the scrimshaw, all exist just by chance, with no intelligent, Skillful Agent involved?"

They sat in silence for a moment, and Adam continued, "Only because of your presuppositions. And we don't know that those are true. That's what I'm finding out in my God-Quest, Skip. God is that intelligent, Skillful Agent. And we can know him! You can know him!"

Skip said nothing as he left the room, but he meditated on this exchange for several days.

Chapter 22: A Modest Proposal

On the one-year anniversary of the plane crash, Adam was in the rhythm of work at TR and growing in his faith at Biblical Community Church with Rev. No-Bull. But Diana wondered if he was losing interest in her. They were always doing things together. They went to the rodeo, both in Mesquite and in Fort Worth. They went line dancing twice and to professional baseball and football games. And they were consistently faithful in participating in the life of Biblical Community Church.

One year and one day after the plane crash that ended Caroline's life and began Adam's God-Quest, Diana had become so impatient with Adam's romantic progress, she decided to help him. She said, "Adam, I don't want you to ever leave me."

Adam disingenuously said, "I've no plans to go anywhere, Diana."

"I'm trying to tell you that I want to spend my whole life with you, Adam."

He continued with this line of teasing, "What do you propose, M'Lady?"

"I'd like for us to have children."

"I'm not sure what you're trying to say to me, Diana. Don't be cryptic. What are you trying to tell me?"

"Let me put it in words even you can understand: I think it's God's will for us to marry."

He said, "Each other?"

She hit him, and then he kissed her, and Diana said, "Is that a proposal?"

"Let's talk about it. What do you have in mind? Do you really think God wants us to marry—each other?"

"I think so. I know I want us to marry, each other." Their wedding was not as grand or as showy as Adam's baptismal celebration. They had a church wedding at BCC with Frank officiating. Esperanza was the Matron of Honor, and Skip was Adam's Best Man. They rented a cabin at a campground in Oklahoma and biked and hiked their way through a week long honeymoon.

Skip was not thrilled with being in a church, but he had lost some of his atheistic dogmatism and was convinced that Adam's experience was genuine.

Esperanza had Juan's baby—well he was three months old now—she had named Juan Marcos Reyes and called him Marc. That same day, Adam took a box of cash from his safe to Edward Jones and invested all of it— several thousand dollars— in Juan Marcos Reyes' name for his college education.

Every year on the anniversary of Caroline's funeral, Adam and Diana went to the cemetery and put flowers on Caroline's grave and on Juan's grave. They also took Esperanza and Marc to Juan's grave, and Adam repeats for Marc what a great man and friend his father was.

Adam and Diana became close friends with Jack and Susan Blake, often doing things together.

Without consulting Skip or TR's attorney, Adam met with the Hayes— the couple who were suing TR. Their meeting began with some tension, but the more they talked, the more the argument sounded like a conversation. All parties agreed to submit the lawsuit to arbitration. Frank put Adam in touch with a member of BCC who agreed to serve as Adam's arbiter, and the Hayes selected a person to serve as an arbiter for them. The two arbiters selected a third person to join them as an arbitration team.

For the next few days, the arbitration team read documents, including the National Association of Realtors booklet on business ethics. Adam and the Hayes signed a document agreeing to abide by the decision of the three-person arbitration team as the case began.

The arbiters planned a meeting at the Hayes residence for a Saturday morning. Adam told Diana that he had to go to a meeting and declined to answer her questions about the meeting.

After an hour of discussion, the team asked the Hayes and Adam to leave the room while they discussed the case. Within 20 minutes, the team invited them to return.

Before 11:00 a.m., everyone—all three arbiters, the Hayes, and Adam agreed that TR was culpable—Adam agreed to the penalty the arbitration team suggested and assured them all that on Monday, he would take a check to the Hayes.

Adam's move to settle this lawsuit annoyed Skip, but he said almost nothing about it. But it made him wonder if his work at TR was coming to an end. In the past, he and Adam always discussed problems like this. *Why did Adam take it on himself to solve this problem with arbitration rather than in court? He didn't save much money by choosing arbitration.*

At the end of TR's fiscal year, Skip and Adam spent a few hours looking over the books. "Skip, let's review and evaluate the past months of applying biblical ethical principles to Terry Relators. Interrupt. Interject. Ask questions. As needed.

"First, Terry Realtor's profits are up twelve percent over last year."

"Good."

"Second, Terry Realtor's share of the market in our service area is growing."

"Good."

"Third, Terry Realtor's reputation among real estate companies in our market is up. We are the leading realty in our market—in both domestic and commercial properties."

"All good." Now, how would you rate the morale of our sales staff?"

"It's also even better than it was."

"Great. I thought so too, and I'm glad we agree."

"So what should TR do? Go back to the way we used to do business? Or continue following God's leadership?"

Skip did not hesitate, He said, "The latter", but it lacked enthusiasm. Adam noticed that Skip would not even say '*God.*'

"I agree, not because business is better, but because we are trusting and obeying God. We will continue. And Skip, I think you're doing a great job as Sales Manager."

"Thanks, Adam. I think you're doing a pretty good job as a Christian, too."

"Skip, I can hardly wait until you come to trust the Lord too."

"Yeah, well don't hold your breath."

"Skip, you don't want to compete with The Almighty." And Adam laughed.

About the Author

Born in a suburb north of Boston, Massachusetts, the youngest of five children, Steve Badger's family moved to Miami, Florida, when he was 9 years old. Later his family moved to the Florida panhandle about 20 miles south of Dothan, Alabama, and three years later (in 1960) to Hattiesburg, Mississippi.

As a youngster of about 7-years old, Steve repented of his life of sin and confessed faith in Christ Jesus. Later, during his first year of graduate school at USM, he got saved again. Then in 1971, he got saved again. [It may be time for him to get saved again—we'll see.]

He attended Hattiesburg High school, but graduated from FCAHS in Brooklyn. He earned a BS in biology and secondary education from William Carey College and taught science at Sumrall Attendance Center—after successfully completing "student teaching" at Eatonville High School. In 1973, he earned a PhD in chemistry from the University of Southern Mississippi. Twenty-two years after completing his PhD, he earned his first and only master's degree in biblical literature from the Assemblies of God Theological Seminary (1995).

While a student at William Carey, he met and married a petite young lady from Moselle, MS. Then on Thanksgiving Day, 1964, he and Dale Patterson were married at Shelton Baptist Church. In November 2014, they celebrated 50 years of marriage. Dale & Steve had five children: Mark, Hope, twin boys, and Sara. The twin boys were born prematurely and lived an hour or so before they died. Mark was 21 when he was killed in an accident in 1986 and is buried in the cemetery behind Shelton Baptist Church. Hope and Sara are married with children of their own.

After grad school, Steve taught for five years at Jackson State University and spent a few summers doing scientific research in government research laboratories (USDA, EPA, National Marine Fisheries Services, a subsidiary of NOAA).

He is an ordained minister with the Assemblies of God and has served as both senior pastor and associate pastor. He has taught and preached in several foreign countries including Bulgaria, South Africa, the Republic of

Congo (Brazzaville), Kenya, Mexico, the Dominican Republic, Cuba, England, southernmost Louisiana, and New Jersey.

From 2001-2013, he taught chemistry at Evangel University (Springfield, MO). His wife's health prompted him to retire in July 2013.

A few years ago, his wife, Dale Patterson Badger, was diagnosed with dementia. She is currently cared for professionally, about 30 miles from where he lives. He and his wife have two adult daughters, two grand-daughters, and a grandson.

For about twelve years, Steve and Evangel University colleague, biologist Mike Tenneson have been researching Christians' attitudes and beliefs about the relationship between Christian faith and the natural sciences (specifically, creation-evolution).

This is Badger's second attempt to write a novel that portrays biblical Christianity. If you find this interesting, you may also like to read *Faith's Crusade*. This and some of his other books are available on Amazon.com.

Real Books & Authors, Real Artists & Music

Bible translations and Their Abbreviations:
New International Version, NIV
New American Standard Bible, NASB
The Living Translation, TLT
Contemporary English Version, CEV

Books Mentioned :
Duvall & Hayes, *Grasping God's Word*
Duvall & Hayes, *Living God's Word*

Gordon D. Fee, NIBC
The Pastoral Epistles: 1 and 2 Timothy, Titus

Gordon Fee & Douglas Stuart
How to Read the Bible for All Its Worth

C.S. Lewis
Surprised by Joy: The Shape of My Early Life.

Wilkins, Michael and J. P. Moreland
Jesus under Fire: Modern Scholarship Reinvents the Historical Jesus.

Musicians and Their Songs
Alison Krauss & Union Station, Live album
"There Is a Reason"

The Moody Blues, "Seventh Sojourn" album
"Lost in a Lost World"
"I'm Just a Singer (In a Rock and Roll Band)"

Chris Tomlin
"How Great Is Our God"